MY
FATHER'S
DIET

My Father's Diet

ADRIAN NATHAN WEST

SHEFFIELD – LONDON – NEW YORK

First published in 2022 by And Other Stories
Sheffield – London – New York
www.andotherstories.org

1 3 5 7 9 8 6 4 2

ISBN: 9781913505226
eBook ISBN: 9781913505233

Editor: Jeremy M. Davies; Copy-editor: Jane Haxby; Proofreader: Sarah Terry; Typeset in
Albertan Pro and Linotype Syntax by Tetragon, London; Cover Design: Tom Etherington;
Printed and bound on acid-free, age-resistant Munken Premium by CPI Limited, Croydon, UK.

And Other Stories gratefully acknowledge that our work is supported
using public funding by Arts Council England.

For Beatriz

1

My father—my real father, whom I rarely saw throughout my childhood, because my mother divorced him when I was two, and he'd moved to the Midwest to make something of himself—was tall, with a splayed, reclining stance that brought prominence to his round belly. His large, gold-framed glasses gave his eyes a tint of amber. They rested halfway down an unusually shaped nose like a seahorse's snout, with an initial, broad bow rising up between the caruncles, then turning in briefly on itself before flourishing in a soft, almost square bump. His glasses seemed always to be falling off, to have gotten smudged; or one stem would be tucked cleanly behind his ear while the other had wandered up the side of his head; or else the plastic pads on the bridge piece would have bent, so that they sat at an angle on his face, giving him the aspect of a drunkard or the loser in a fight. They caused him a lot of trouble, and were as often in his hands as on his face. His long, flat fingers would polish the lens with a fold of shirttail, or slide a milky-colored nail into the screw; if it pulled away from the cuticle, my father would bellow and put it in his mouth, and the glasses would have to be sent off to the shop.

While away, he finished an advanced degree, the acquisition of which was a source of such pride that on his address labels and credit cards and even the message that greeted callers when he was away from his phone, the honorific *doctor* always preceded his name. Once or twice, to excuse his long absence, he complained of the poverty of opportunities available in the 1980s in the city of my birth. He had wanted more for himself, he claimed, among other things because he hoped to offer me more of what he called *chances* that he'd never had himself. But my mother always avowed that his disappearance had nothing to do with ambition. When I was a baby, the two of them had gone to a party, she told me several times, at the home of a musician friend of my father's, and she had opened a bathroom door to find my father with his pants around his knees and a woman acquaintance in a similar state of undress. My mother turned and ran off screaming, and my father chased her, holding up his trousers and swearing that it wasn't what it looked like. My mother would laugh at this stage of the story, which was one of her favorites, squeezing her eyelids into jaded slivers and blowing twin tapers of cigarette smoke from her nose.

I have only two memories of him from before he left. Once, getting me ready for day care, he tried to strip me of my favorite red corduroys, which I had been wearing all week, and to force me into another pair that I hated, of a dull moss green that even in the early 1980s had already fallen out of fashion. "Goddamn it, you'll mind me," he said as he held me down. Another time, attracted by its bright, mysterious tip, smoldering under a crust of white ash, I took one of his cigars from the glass ashtray, touched it to my belly button, and began to howl and heave as my skin cooked and welted. My mother yelled at my father for leaving me alone with it, and he protested that he'd been gone only a second.

He seldom returned home, and when he did, I might not see him. There were a few breaks from school when he pulled up in his small red sedan to take me away for a disheartening weekend with his parents. Otherwise I knew him only from the fairly affected-looking photographs, posed with some implement of the holidays—a paper turkey, a gleaming cardboard heart, or a white Santa's beard that hid his face—that arrived every few years with a box of candy or a toy.

I visited him twice out West that I remember. The first time, he was single, and lived in an apartment with a private entrance and stairway on the second story of a family home with wooden siding painted a dull rust brown. He had a claw-foot tub of tarnished copper, and the water flowed into it not from the tap but from a slender plastic tube. Once it had filled to just over my thighs, he left me alone there to tend to his papers. There was something tempting in the sinuosity of that fluted white hose, and when I reached out to touch it, it leapt into the air and twirled in circles like a maddened serpent. I was horrified; I half-hopped, half-scooted backward, slipped and struck my head, and screamed until he ran back in to save me.

The second time he was living with a woman with cropped, curly hair who worked as a nurse in a hospital. We went there late one night to pick her up after she'd been called in, and I saw an insane person in the waiting area, both his hands wrapped in bloody bandages. It was a cold, dry winter then, and we hardly went outside for most of my stay, but one day a neighbor, a friend of my father's, dragged me through the icy streets on a tire tied to the bumper of his truck. Otherwise I stayed by the fireplace reading and drawing pictures in a sketchbook while my father sat studying in an easy chair.

My mother sought, if not frantically, then with admirable persistence amid adversity, a replacement for him—I hesitate here to use the word *suitable*, in light of these men's often-lavish imperfections. It was never clear which among these was a suitor and which a mere *friend*, and nothing remains of them to me but casual traits that have turned caricaturesque beneath the soot of memory: the man with the mustache whose image, when I call it to mind, I cannot think of separately from those novelty glasses with the attached bushy eyebrows and plastic nose that people pretended to find funny in the seventies and eighties; the one who drove the van covered in spray-painted squiggles denouncing fluoridated water or perhaps the IRS; the balloon artist with an unspecified cerebronervous affliction that caused him great difficulty pronouncing certain words; the radio repairman who lived with his father and had shot himself in the stomach as a teenager. This last had a cluster of sunken scars on his abdomen and couldn't eat foods containing milk or butter. My mother was unlucky in love. It can't have helped that her only avocation was throwing darts in a taproom within walking distance of our home that did not cater to what is known as an exclusive clientele. Her good fortune, if it was that, in meeting the man I would later take to calling the Weirdo lay in her decision to take me there at lunchtime on a holiday, to satisfy my craving for one of the flat, greasy, overdone cheeseburgers the place produced between the hours of eleven in the morning and four in the afternoon. The Weirdo was a teetotaler, and he was there only because he was laying tile in a tanning salon in the U-shaped shopping center with the mystifying name "Arcadian Village" that shared a parking lot with the bar.

The Weirdo was a surly-faced man, short and stubby, with a beard, twenty years or so my mother's junior (I never knew his real age, which he concealed with reference to a hatred for birthdays, a hand-me-down from his Jehovah's Witness parents; and unlike most adults, he had no box or file folder containing birth certificate, tax returns, or any other documents bearing indications of his past or provenance). Due to their difference in age, my mother called him her *sweat puppy* among the friends she would cease to see once their relationship began in earnest, and this term, which I had never heard another person use before and have never heard since, seemed to me, judging by the pursed lips of these women as they sipped their Sea Breezes and Harvey Wallbangers through straws, indicative of his sexual potency or endurance. Then again, he boasted of the same on one of their early nights together, when I was in my bedroom and presumed to be asleep, and he spent hours trying to cajole my mother into bed while he played the martial arts video game *Karateka* on the computer she had purchased for me on a whim ten years before computers could do anything useful: "I may not look like much, but I swear to God, in the sack I'm a stallion," he told her. I don't know why my mother was reluctant just then, but within days, he overcame her resistance. I remember my mother's panting through the wall separating our bedrooms, like the heaves of a person on the verge of vomiting. The rhythm of it I didn't understand, because, though my mother had answered me plainly when I asked her at age five where babies came from, she had used the unfortunate verb *place—the man places his penis inside the woman*—and for many years, I assumed the two lovers remained stationary after insertion.

The Weirdo had an incomprehensible surname, the sound of which, as he uttered it, must have little resembled its pronunciation in the land of his ancestors. "I'm Irish enough to get mad fast and Russian enough to stay that way," he liked to say with unfathomable swagger. But judging from the profusion of consonants in his patronymic, I think he must actually have been Georgian. His father, a mechanic, had pulled his own teeth with a pair of pliers to avoid paying for a trip to the dentist; his mother, a white-haired, fine-toothed woman, had a horrible collection of paint-by-numbers clowns. I met his parents when he and my mother had been together for less than a year and were aping an ordinary courtship; the pretense was soon enough abandoned, and when they purchased their land—they were already talking about it during their first days together, and were soon gripped by the notion of the freedom it would supposedly bring them—their few social contacts withered to none.

The move to this land prompted the only serious consideration of living with my father I ever entertained as a minor. At first, the idea of a new home was hardly less invigorating to me than to my mother and the Weirdo. Their cow-eyed mentions of the property's "fully stocked pond" never persuaded me of the charms of killing fish as a hobby; and the pride the two of them seemed to take in "having something we can call our own" struck me even then as a mere abstraction; but, since the Weirdo had moved in, seven months after they started dating, my room had been repurposed to house what we loosely called his tools— which ranged from dismantled televisions to heat lamps for the raising of serpents—and I was made to use the couch as my bed. I could not sleep there, because in the evening, the Weirdo liked to engage me in what he called "philosophical discussions," most of them touching the morality of waging nuclear war against impoverished populations he deemed "useless." A room of my own, in a house rather than an apartment, offered the promise of relief. What they did not tell me, minimizing the length of the drive as people do in places where a car is a necessity, was that the land lay an hour from town, from my school, and from my friends; nor did they reveal, before taking me to see it the first time, that the house there was only approximately a house. The roof was sunken in one place, and soil was visible between cracks in the floorboards, which had been set directly over the joists with no plywood or insulation in between. My room-to-be was in an unfinished A-frame garret on the second floor of the garage, where the previous owners had stored their children's old toys and outgrown clothes. "This is cool, isn't it?" my mother said. "We'll clear this out and put in the Sheetrock and carpet and it'll be like your own little castle." I thought then of the small plot surrounding the trailer the Weirdo was sharing with his sister when my mother met him, with its scattering of projects in various stages of incompletion: the wreck of an apple-green sports coupe, its engine rusting alongside it; tires amassed for some obscure purpose; a basketball backboard without a hoop; a spike set in concrete with attached collar and chain for a dog that must have run away or died—and I doubted whether sufficient initiative existed to make this space adequate for me, and envisioned endless days of walking around the property, bored and alone.

That night, impulsively, I told my mother I wanted to leave, that I would ask my father to let me go live with him. For a moment, she said nothing. The smoker's wrinkles tautened around her lips. Hunched over in the blue wing chair with the brown cigarette burn on the armrest, the Weirdo folded his hands and stared down into his palms. On TV, a man in black robes was adjudicating a dispute between neighbors, one of whom had borrowed the other's lawnmower and was suing for damages after cutting off half of his own foot. For viewers—and my mother was a devoted one—the judge's charisma lay in his inexhaustible store of outrage at the contending parties' allegations, often phrased in folky chestnuts like "That dog won't hunt" or "Boy, you're dumber than a mud fence." It made me want to scream.

She next asked me simply, "Have you really thought about this?"

"The house is in the middle of nowhere," I said.

"That's the point, some peace and quiet. A place where we can do whatever we like. Plus, it's a real house, with space. We can't just buy something like that anywhere."

"Nobody's parents are going to drive them an hour to come see me."

"It's not an hour."

"Yes, it is."

Here the Weirdo intervened, reaching his crooked index finger as close to my face as he could, calling me "Boy," and telling me to respect my mother. I objected that I did respect her, that this had nothing to do with respect, and that I had to wonder if they respected me. Neither of them had asked my thoughts about the move until the decision was taken. "Be careful," the Weirdo said, cutting me off. "You're soon to get out of pocket."

I walked to the kitchen, where the phone hung on the far wall, stretched the cord into the pantry closet, and shut the door to call my grandmother. My father's number I didn't know, hadn't known for years; I'd had no cause to speak with him; and from what I knew, he moved often, in and out of student housing and between smaller and larger apartments depending on the receipt or denial of grants and loans. My grandmother didn't pick up, and I burst into tears. I was silent at first, then I sank down, pressed my feet into the back wall, and started stomping and lamenting—in words, I think, but I only recall making incoherent groans—until the Weirdo came in, jerked me in the air by my biceps, carried me down the hall, kicked me twice in the backside, and threw me onto the bed. My mother told me afterward he had cried through the night, but hadn't known what else to do.

2

When my father graduated, he returned to his home state, but to a city a hundred miles from ours, and later, to a small town equally far away, but to the east. I have no impression of his person at the time, only of the spaces he inhabited: spare, always scrupulously clean, everything wiped down several times a day with glass cleaner; more human than a furniture showroom but less so than a home, with no evidence of the peculiarity a life almost inevitably gathers around itself but his pile of *Playboy* magazines and his king-size waterbed with brown vinyl railings. For years, he went from job to job, hovering in the same geography, now an hour away, now two, whether in a roundabout attempt to get closer to me or from reluctance to definitively return I am not sure.

I would not say his proximity brought us together. Now and then, he retrieved me to spend the night with him, but we never knew what to talk about, living in ignorance of each other's daily lives, and would sit in near silence until the tension grew insufferable, and he would put two Hungry Man dinners in the oven and turn on *Miami Vice* or *Mike Hammer*. When he finally got hired in the city I lived in, he took up with a horrible, pug-nosed woman from Massachusetts or New Hampshire who resented my occasional visits and rarely allowed me to leave my room—the guest room, rather, with its foldout couch, rolltop desk, and black-and-white TV. For a while, then, my father made a spirited attempt to convince me to live with him. The impetus was not so much love or a sense of paternal duty as jealousy and fear of usurpation. He had hoped, it seems, with a mannish firm handshake, to establish some rapport with the Weirdo, but after their initial meeting, when the latter had turned around without a word after my father's overture—"Maybe we can get a beer sometime"—the Weirdo would hide away in the garage no sooner than he saw my father's car turn down our road.

Reasons abounded for holding the Weirdo in suspicion—he was racist, he beat the dogs, and though he never raised his hands against me after the night I threatened to move away, he made it known that he felt recourse to violence against me was his right as an adult—but my father had no notion of any of this. His distaste for the Weirdo was rather aesthetic: a stubby, short-fingered man who rarely washed, and then only badly, the Weirdo had grease streaks on his T-shirts and tears in his jeans, spoke in a laconic, woodsy patois, and used the word "ideal" when he meant "idea." He smoked marijuana, as my father discovered apparently by digging through our trash, and for a year or two, there was the threat of a custody battle hinging on this supposed infamy; but whether because the pug-nosed wife decided in the end that she didn't want me living with them or because my father himself reconsidered the financial burden I might represent—"If he doesn't like paying his child support, he damn sure won't like keeping you in food and clothes," my mother said at the time—the threat subsided. It was arranged that my father could "have" me every

17

weekend, but after a few months the drive became tiresome to him. Every weekend ebbed into every other, and when I got a job at sixteen, I started spending Friday and Saturday nights with a friend who lived near work, and eventually stopped seeing him at all.

I didn't say goodbye to him when I left for college. I didn't call him when I dropped out and moved home after just two quarters. My intention was to stay at home and work as much overtime as possible, save money, and go away to New York or Paris, two cities I'd never visited but that seemed to represent the fulfillment of a series of long-nurtured though elusive dreams; but my mother impressed upon me the necessity of getting my degree at all costs. Her urgings were buttressed by the Weirdo, who told me flatly: "Boy, you need to learn something you can do with your brain. You ain't me, I can make a living with my hands, I can do masonry, I can plumb. You don't got the damnedest idea of all that."

"I've worked in restaurants since I was sixteen. I can do that wherever," I replied.

"Sure. Some ambition," the Weirdo said.

"Is what you do better?"

The Weirdo's eyes bulged, the blood rose to his face from beneath his ring-neck T-shirt, and he sucked in a rasping breath. My mother, seeing the blue cable of vein squiggle in the center of his forehead, butted in to bring the conversation to a close: "Just get the damned degree and you can figure out what you want to do with your life later." When the summer ended, I found a room in an apartment downtown through an ad in the newspaper and enrolled at a small branch college attached to the state university system.

And so I hardly knew my father when I received a mawkish letter in my mailbox, around Thanksgiving of that second freshman year, in which he expressed his regret that we had "drifted so far apart." He recounted a series of tender moments from my infancy that I didn't remember. "Knowing what I know now," he wrote, "I can't believe your mother and I couldn't have worked things out." He told me of a recurring dream of his, in which I was once more a little boy, and I'd slipped into a pond and he was trying to save me, but he couldn't see me, because the green water was opaque. He thrust his hand through the ripples on the surface, but pulled up only silt and milfoil. "Every time that happens, I wake up in a sweat," he wrote. He apologized for the time he'd spent with the woman from Massachusetts or New Hampshire, whom he had left some time ago. It hadn't been easy, but it was for the best. "You think after you get your PhD, everything's going to be cake and roses"—he used this odd turn of phrase instead of the more typical *sunshine and roses*—"but the truth is you're still starting from nothing." Lamenting that he had missed a good deal of my life, he acknowledged that it was unlikely we could "pick up where we left off." But he wanted me to know he was *there*, and that we might embark on a new relationship. He concluded with the words, "Hoping to get reacquainted," then "Love," then "Your father."

I called him the next night. After ten minutes' conversation, during which the two of us avoided his written affirmations in favor of small talk about sports and politics, matters of intermediate importance that touched only slightly on one another's lives, we set a lunch date at a chain restaurant in a shopping center for the following week.

I arrived first and was sitting in a booth, flicking through a series of laminated cardboard sheets hung on a plastic frame touting specialty drinks in otherworldly colors, the splendors of the salad bar, and mucky desserts served in frosted, oversized martini glasses, when he walked in. My father was dressed in four shades of brown—beige blazer, taupe turtleneck, khaki slacks, and boat shoes (without socks) the color of ferrous clay. He brought with him a new wife, whose existence he had failed to mention. She had dry black hair that framed her face in a succession of hooked billows descending from a pale blue, vermiform part. In her cheeks was the indelible, grainy blush of the experienced alcoholic. After our waitress's two-minute harangue, which comprised a welcome, an exchange of names, a list of specials, and an elaborate and clearly hard-to-remember pledge about the sort of service she hoped to provide, my father ordered a gin and tonic and his wife a Chardonnay. I had a coffee. I was not yet twenty-one.

With an expression of vague and inordinate solicitousness, my father asked, "So what happened last year?" I did not know how to answer. I didn't want to tell him about my girlfriend in college, our breakup, my depression there, or my decision to leave—chided as *running away* by my mother, the Weirdo, and more than one friend—just to see if that sadness might lift. I didn't want to talk about my troubled sleep or the urge to flee from nothing in particular that came upon me at the oddest hours, but especially when it was bright out, and the sun seemed a challenge or affront. It would all have felt like a confession of inadequacy, or simply stupid, but I was no less repelled by the ready-made explanations available to me, meant to evoke automatic sympathy, such as *I was having suicidal thoughts* or *I was struggling with anxiety.* And so I told my father I had wanted to study French, and that the department there was lacking, that none of the professors specialized in the modern literature that most interested me. This was absurd, as the out-of-state university was much larger than the one at home, and I had two years of core classes to take before beginning my major.

"What are you going to do with French?" he asked, and again, I was at a loss, because my only ambition, from early youth, had been to go *somewhere else*, and I had chosen that language, in which my grades were execrable, based on a superficial familiarity with the country, which I envisioned in terms of somewhat farcical symbols—trench coats, rococo interiors, espresso in demitasses, the filterless Gitanes an acquaintance had brought back from a family trip to several European capitals. I thought—despite my lassitude—that one day, through as-yet-to-be-determined means, I might become a person of culture, and that when this occurred, the French language would be of use to me.

"I might take the civil service exam," I said.

This explanation seemed to satisfy my father, and his wife, suddenly thrilled, told me how *marvelous* the experience of travel could be. "I was in Africa for several years," she said. "But we didn't study French there, I learned German."

After a streak of introductory phrases—*Hallo, wie geht's, wie viel Uhr ist es*—she fell into an apparent fit of glossolalia, emitting a mishmash of nasal vowels interspersed with trills and murmurs, the odd proper word bobbing to the surface like a soup bone in a pot of roiling broth, then finished with a row of what began as real numbers and transformed into a semblance of monotones in Mandarin or Cantonese: "*Eins, zwei, drei, hai, lai, kai, sai.*"

"Wow," I said.

"Where ya livin'?" my father asked with the folksy pronunciation he lapsed into when he was ill at ease.

"Downtown."

"Solo or with a roommate?"

"I share with this girl, she's a student too."

"Is she your *giiiirlfriend*?" his wife asked trochaically, ending in a near laugh and flushing, as if the prospect excited her.

"No. Actually I think she's scared of me or something. She just spends all her time in her room."

"I'm sure you didn't go through a whole year of college without going out with anyone, though, right?" my father asked.

I thought of Fox, of her green eyes ringed in badly applied mascara, the way the fine fuzz beside her ears pushed through her base makeup, how a finer streak of the same makeup overlay each one; of her hair, which changed color almost weekly, and was sometimes mussed and sometimes hugged her skull in braids; and of her presence, at once hard to picture and far more palpable than these isolated details.

"Yeah, I was seeing someone, but I moved, so that was kind of that."

The waitress returned with our drinks and asked, "Are y'all ready?" Everything on the menu was fried or *smothered* with cheese, and this frying and smothering and lathering, all those oleaginous descriptors with which the very glossy illustrated menu induced one to try what was, in the light of reason, a horrifying array of confections—Asian Spiced Tamales, Bacon-Ranch Country Fried Sirloin—already contained, in miniature, some essential aspect of the life I believed I wished to escape. Believed, I say, because I was unfamiliar with any other sort of

22

life as a reality outside of a small private canon of books and films, which offered themselves less as a model of vital possibilities than as objects of devotion or the raw material of dreams in the years when I had yet to even take an airplane.

"I'll just have a Caesar salad," I said.

"Is that all?" my father asked.

"But you're so thin!" his wife averred.

I shrugged and sat still while my father ordered a burger, the "Barbecue Beef Bonanza," and a shrimp scampi for his wife. "If you'd like to add cheese to that, we have Jack, Swiss, Cheddar, American, Provolone, goat cheese, or mozzarella," the waitress informed my father, before encouraging him to add a soup or salad for only a dollar ninety-nine. His wife's entrée came with a salad for which various bonus garnishments were offered, but she limited herself to Thousand Island dressing.

"Where did you live in Africa?" I asked her once the waitress had left us in peace.

"Namibia. In Tsumeb at first, and then in Windhoek for a couple of years."

I tried to imagine these places, neither of which I had heard of, but the only notions that came to me were whitewashed buildings, red, windblown soil, and dark, thin people in ornately woven garments conjured up vaguely, I assume, from a documentary or magazine.

"What did you do there?"

"Well, it changed after a while. My father was in mining. Metallurgy. So at first he was actually down in the mines there in Tsumeb. But then he started moving up in the company and they put him in management in the capital. I went to high school there and everything, it was really a big part of my life, but then—"

"How's work?" my father asked, exasperated with her story.

"It's fine. It's work. What about yours?"

"Well, we'll have to see, won't we?" he laughed. He explained that he had just taken a new position as human resources director for a large insurance conglomerate. "I mean, the money's right," he said warily, "but money isn't everything. I still haven't gotten a feel for the people there, how the ship runs, you really have to be there for a bit to catch all that. But I'm looking forward to it. Really I need it to work out, we've put a lot of eggs in that basket. Starting over at this point would be a major pain."

"Where are you staying now?"

"Hell, we're in a damn hotel, if you believe that."

"Why?"

"Well, we're selling the old place, I don't know if you ever saw it, the bungalow up on the ridge. And it just worked out that the buyer had to move in ASAP and the family in the place we bought ended up needing a bit more time, I guess they had problems scheduling their movers or something."

"I like it," his wife said. "Room service, Jacuzzi bathtub, I think it's wonderful."

"Yeah, it's great for the old wallet, too," said my father, who had a predilection for referring to places and objects as *old*, and spoke of trips to the old grocery store, breaking out the old weed whacker, and so forth.

"Oh, we can afford it," she replied.

"So what do you do at the job?" I asked my father.

"HR," he said. He went on to explain that human resources was a department with many facets, requiring an acquaintance both with the company's changing needs, in order to locate ideal candidates for open positions, and with the complexities of employment law. He would have a large staff, and would have to instill in them the culture of the parent corporation, which had recently bought my father's firm from its local owners. Periodically he stopped speaking and took sips from his drink, and once, his wife interrupted him in a way that made clear she hadn't followed the conversation; he looked at her scornfully, and she blushed and stared down into her glass of wine. My father tried to ignore her, then, in a show of indulgence, turned to the side and presented her with a close-eyed, toothy smile, his top lip scrolling up to reveal his gums—like a rat nibbling a piece of cheese, my mother had said in an uncharitable moment. To allay the tension, I asked her how they'd met.

"At a conference," my father said.

"In Indianapolis. I just thought your father was so refined. You know, most of the people at these things are just—ugh. You know, just boring guys with bald spots and clip-on ties."

"Excuse me," my father said with a mock-withering look, pointing to the pink pinnacle of his scalp.

"Oh. Well, you know how to tie a tie, at least," she said, and tousled his delicately arranged hairs. "And anyway, we were at one of these presentations in the ballroom of the hotel, I didn't know anyone there, and your father just came up and asked if he could sit with me. And I was like sure, and he's very funny, he was joking around and the speaker wasn't very interesting, and the next thing I know he's asking me on a date. We went to a *Moroccan* restaurant, it was incredible, you had to eat with your hands, we had couscous, uh, lamb, I think. I'd never even had lamb before."

"Did you live far away?" I asked.

"Oh, not too far," she replied. "I mean we had both had to travel to the conference. It turned out we were about an hour and a half from each other. But that was OK, we'd see each other on the weekends, and then eventually I just left my job to go stay with him, he said there was no point in our going back and forth like that, he loved me, and we didn't need a second income, and I thought, well, might as well try it, you know."

"Biggest mistake I ever made," said my father after two baritone chuckles, and his wife said, "Shut up!" and slapped him on the shoulder.

When our meals were over, my father and I refused dessert, but his wife ordered a strawberry cheesecake, or something alleged to be so, invisible beneath stelliform strips of canned whipped cream, maraschino cherries, sauces, and sugared nuts. "Well, hell, if you're going to get that, I'm going to have another drink," my father said. His eyes were glassing over, and when his wife spoke too long without addressing him, he slunk back in the booth and took several long, deep breaths.

Regaling no one in particular with the words, "Oh, wow, oh my God, this is amazing," his wife spooned the sloppy mass into her mouth, insensible for some time of my father's stupor. When she was done, she laid her spoon on a bar napkin.

"You all right there, soldier?" she asked him.

"I'm fine," my father said, miffed, refusing to believe he had fallen asleep.

3

Two weeks later, they moved into a single-story home on a quarter-acre plot of land in a development of identical houses on curving streets of which the promotional pamphlet my father showed me boasted, "It has the quiet of the country with the convenience of easy access to the city." The house had a screened-in porch his wife soon took for her own, furnishing it with a sofa and colorful cushions, a wicker coffee table, and a stereo, and adorning the walls with dark wooden masks and other African kitsch. When I came over, she would be sitting there smoking a tiny pipe or drinking a glass of red wine and listening to drum music; she would pause the CD, wave me over, and tell me to listen, providing me with some detail about the musician or the provenance of the instruments that I immediately forgot. Occasionally she would take out the liner notes and read to me from the translations of the lyrics. I never managed to appreciate them.

My father proposed we make a tradition of Sunday dinners together, and I agreed to attend when I wasn't working. I went there maybe a dozen times. My father would cook the meat outside while his wife prepared vegetables and accompaniments over the stove. Two or three times he handed me a beer, a Courage Best Bitter. The brand seemed to have some significance for him: he said its name aloud whenever he opened one, either because he thought it was distinguished or because he had happy memories of it—I never asked and was never told. After we had clinked the necks of the bottles, he would invite me to join him outside and "fire up the old grill." The steaks or pork he retrieved from the refrigerator where they lay in a zippable bag filled with reduced-sodium marinade and dry spices, and when he laid them across the griddle, the liquid dripped down and crackled on the coals, sending flames to head-height. While my father stabbed at the victuals with a two-pronged fork and the juice spurted, sizzling from the wound, I would look down at the brown crabgrass that stuck up around the soles of my shoes, or gaze past the storage shed, built to resemble a red barn, to the pinewoods beyond the fences enclosing the backyards of the houses.

At some point I would grow bored and say I had to go to the bathroom. When his wife looked at me on the way in, smiling as if wanting to converse, I would point down the hall to the wooden door. Its dull blue paint had been sanded away purposely to give it what people call a "farmhouse look." Locking myself away, I would pee, run the water to cover the sound of my movements, and rifle through their belongings. Beyond a quantity of unfathomable creams and hair products, more of them my father's than hers, there was little of intrigue save for a stack of creased paperbacks by beatnik novelists, one of which had a postcard of William Burroughs as a bookmark, looking cadaverous and irritable under his fedora. On the back was a message to someone with a strange nickname, Bear or Moose, saying, "Tell my captain that I love him." I put the card in my pocket, and for some months it sat on my windowsill before disappearing into some box or other that I have subsequently thrown out. The books, I was later told, had been the property of this Bear or Moose, a friend who had lived in the wife's previous home for the last six months of his life before dying of cancer of the pancreas.

Around eight, the meal would be laid on the table, with plates over place mats, pewter flatware, and fringed napkins of checked cloth rolled and stuffed into wooden rings. A bottle of wine would appear after the salad, and my father would struggle to remove the cork before pouring himself a taste, swirling it in his glass, and declaring it "very fine indeed." He would offer to let me sample it, as though to raise me to some ideal of gourmandise, and we would set into the main course. My father rarely spoke. His attention was consumed with cutting his food into small, orderly bites that he would bring to his mouth and chew with almost mechanical regularity. I would ask his wife about her time in Africa, which she would have brought up anyway, it being the only subject that enthused her; and she would inquire into my interests or my opinions on whatever news she could recall from the morning's broadcast. She was painfully long-winded, and would agree effusively with whatever I said to her, even if I'd hoped to disagree; and my attempts to make myself plain, amid her tortuous rejoinders and backpedaling, grew so bewildering and dull that I was glad for my father to interrupt with some anecdote from the local newspaper or the *New Yorker*. Late in the meal, my father would remove his glasses, inspecting them for a spell, maybe blowing on them and wiping them, before laying them upside down next to the bread basket. His wife liked to pay homage to my father's erudition, saying she'd always hoped to be with an *intellectual*; and when she did so, he would lean against the backrest of his chair, shut his eyes, and flatten one hand on the table along the rim of his plate, while with the other he serenely stroked his nose.

At the time I lived in a dingy gray brick building dating back to the turn of the century. My roommate, a nutrition student, was a twenty-year-old blonde who would scurry to her room like a roach whenever I opened the door. Her existence for me hardly extended beyond the scuffing of her saddle oxfords on her way out the door in the mornings, her rare trips to the toilet, the flushing followed by the hiss of disinfectant spray, and the lists she left on the counter asking me to buy things for the apartment, all of which I thought trivial and even worthy of contempt, expressing as they did a longing for a domestic order I had never known and did not care to acquire: a can crusher for the garbage, plastic hooks for hanging pot holders, jars to be filled decoratively with cereal or dried legumes.

I slept there, spent my mornings on campus, and in the evenings washed dishes at a beer hall three or four nights a week. I had hoped to become a server, I had thought I was showing initiative with my willingness to start at the bottom, but my managers took my acceptance of the worst and lowest-paid job as a sign that it was the one I was best suited for. My free time I spent walking the grid of streets between the town and the river, anticipating poetic or philosophical inspirations to be jotted down in a leatherette pocket journal. When I had money, I would make a reservation at a so-called *trattoria*, its walls hung with rusted nautical and farm utensils, where I would drink a bottle of mineral water and eat a bowl of pasta and a loaf of bread, trying conspicuously between bites to read whatever book then seemed best to represent my intellectual pretensions. Though I already knew the waitresses there, several of whom were classmates, I always hoped there would be a new one who would notice me, be intrigued, and offer some observation that would lead to love, or at least to sex or one of its preludes. On my way home, I would stop at the Glass Peacock, a wood-paneled dive bar with tic-tac-toe games and obscene mottos etched into the chairs and tabletops. After producing a fake license and handing it to the doorman—I had bought the frayed document from a friend of a friend who hardly resembled me save for the same dismal hairline—I would buy a black beer and drink it on the terrace, ashing my cigarette from the parapet, eyes lost in the scant, scattered orange lights of downtown. When I was broke, I subsisted on canned tuna and brown rice, which grew so repugnant over time that I started washing bites of them down with sips of water from the tap, trying to swallow without chewing.

I was a poor student, despite frequent pledges to myself to do better. The first semester at the new school, I enrolled in six classes, thinking I would make up for lost ground; two months in, I had dropped everything but French, Asian-American Literature, and Astronomy, which I was failing. I kept all of this a secret from my parents, and even developed a series of routines meant to preserve my impression of myself as a student. At eight each morning, I left my apartment for the library, where I would browse the stacks until it brightened out, then take a nap on one of the sofas. The sight of sunlight, the blue of day, depressed me, and I could stand it only a few minutes before the urge to sleep took hold. I never studied, but when I woke up I would write a list of priorities in my notebook to encourage myself to get "on track." At night, after work, I would stare at my textbook, binder, and star charts, picking up my pen and calculator and setting them back down, bewildered by the most rudimentary assignments. I failed Astronomy, barely passed the other classes, and didn't fulfill my science requirement until three years later, the summer before graduation; but I remained impressed by the image my professor, a man with delicate, downy ears and salt-and-pepper mutton chops, imparted of the soundless constellations, whipping ever outward in an endless night, which made me think, for some reason, of the death throes of Hercules in his envenomed robe. As though mute gawking might impart some further understanding, I used to stand in those months on the second-story deck at dawn and sundown, hours barely distinguishable to the eye, to look past the flocks of birds or bats and stare at the stars shivering regally in their celestial sockets, fading in or out of a sky of shifting blue.

A landscaped lake lay at one end of the campus, home to a gaggle of gray geese and domesticated ducks. When it was overcast but not too cold, I would walk to the pharmacy after my nap and buy a bottle of cough syrup to drink along the way there. By the time I reached the benches circling the water, my legs would be wobbly and my thoughts torpid and disordered. Descending to where the soil grew spongy, I'd lie on my back, feel the stiff grass and weeds poking pleasantly through my shirt, fold my forearm over my eyes, and sniff at the rush-scented, water-scented breezes crowding my nostrils.

At night I had chest pains. If I took a deep breath, I'd feel a pop beneath my heart, and they would cease; then my pulse would race, and I would stare at the trinkets on my shelf, lit by the street lamp past my window, trembling at the notion of my own death. Digestion sounds often echoed through the room from the empty spaces in my abdomen. I suffered at the thought of these inward hollows and the corporal doom they intimated, and longed for a solid body of uniform material, like a doll's.

When sleep approached, my thoughts would stray from these fears and turn to my childhood, to people whose names I had known but could no longer remember, to my old pastimes, which appeared to me in the strangest light. I was different from what I had been, but could not say why or how this should be so. Recalling, as though astonished, my lost affection for a toy or cartoon, in light of my present indifference, I wondered what had changed in the interim. As a teenager, I was argumentative and impassioned, and had even gone to protests—against a nuclear plant or the war in Iraq. Now, any opinion I expressed, even the ones I essayed in my mind, sounded hollow and perfunctory. In high school, I was a frantic reader and treasurer of the film club, and I bought two or three albums a week; now I listened over and over to "Low Life" by Iggy Pop and watched and rewatched a staticky bootleg of *Killer of Sheep* I'd ordered from a video store in Atlanta, not because they held special meaning for me, but rather the opposite: mechanically, like a rosary's click or a ticking clock, they helped restore a stupor it was painful to abandon.

4

My father started calling to confide in me more often, and sometimes fretted at his wife's idleness.

"Don't get me wrong, for my part, I couldn't care less," he'd say. "There's plenty of money, that's not the issue. But I worry about her being cooped up at the house. I mean, she's not got much to do except read and watch TV, she doesn't really have any friends here, and she's the one that made the sacrifice, she up and left everything for me. So I feel a bit responsible for her."

Each time we talked, I asked whether she'd been looking for work. For several weeks, he said she hadn't, before one day proclaiming, with a measure of relief, that she had taken a part-time job with a hospital providing home health care for those too poor, too ill, or too obese to travel into town. During the initial consultation, she and a doctor would evaluate her patients' fitness for various pharmaceutical regimens, and she would check in with them regularly over the subsequent months to monitor the treatments' effectiveness. Her charges were senile or feebleminded from birth, or mentally disabled from huffing gas or drinking grain alcohol filtered through toast, and the profusion of their destitution and hardships gave a picturesque sordor to her workaday complaints. Most of her tales centered on the Ricklers, a benighted family in one of the

hundreds of *hollers* branching out from the unincorporated areas surrounding the city—not towns so much as clusters of pawn shops, gas stations, fast-food restaurants, and pool halls set at ten-mile intervals along the highways, each christened with a quaint-sounding toponym. The family's dimensions were uncertain; beside the matriarch, there was her son Ricky, who lay motionless on a bare mattress unless jolted by a periodic seizure; an adolescent daughter, a hooker, according to my father's wife; and a loose group of men who wandered in and out and might have been brothers or cousins or romantic relations. They were selling their medications, she suspected, and she appealed to their doctor to intervene, but, as it turned out, "these people may not be able to spell, but they sure as hell know how to game the system." The law offered no means of addressing her conjectures. She told us of a day Mrs. Rickler had looked up from a talk show while my father's wife was dressing her suppurating foot to ask, "Did they ever catch that man what shot Reagan?" Another time, she leapt up during her son's examination, yelled "Bastard!" and "Son of a bitch!" and started swinging a broom at a derelict who stumbled through the door asking for "a little sugar."

"I think he meant sex," said my father's wife, "but maybe it was drugs, how am I supposed to know."

At first, she reveled in these stories and laughed as she told them, until tears welled in her crow's feet and rolled down her red cheeks. But soon they dwindled, and bitterness pervaded what few she still told. "The goddamn Ricklers," she began to call them, saying, "I don't know how much longer I can stand this shit." She asked her managers to transfer her, but they denied her request for reasons of seniority. "I work harder than half those people that have been there for a decade," she said. My father told her to leave, that there was no need to give notice, but she refused, telling him, "I didn't get my master's degree so I could depend on a man to support me."

During one visit, a spindly figure, an older son, perhaps, walked into the Ricklers' house in jeans and no shirt. After greeting my father's wife with a "Hello, ma'am," he asked Mrs. Rickler to leave for the evening so he could have his friends over for a party.

"I don't think so," she replied.

"Come on, now," the man said, and Mrs. Rickler shook her head. A screaming match erupted, and my father's wife ran out of the house, though there were two hours left in her shift. A few days later, a local policeman called her to make a statement, and informed her that the man had returned that night with a shotgun and blown holes in the walls and doors. Mrs. Rickler and her son had disappeared. According to her daughter, they had gone to stay with "relatives," but the police were considering foul play.

"God knows how anyone got that fat bastard out of there without killing him, he's got a trach tube, he's epileptic, he can't walk or really talk. She's not what you'd call fit as a fiddle herself."

"Well, I think it's a blessing in disguise," my father said. "You're too smart and too talented to be wasting your time with their nonsense. You keep those people alive and they couldn't give less of a damn about you."

"But that's not the point, is it? I mean you can't really just say, well, you're an ignorant hillbilly and your son's got meth mouth and your daughter has probably sucked off the whole trailer park so I'm just going to let you die because you can't figure out your insulin dosages."

"That's not what I'm saying," my father replied. "But by the same token, shouldn't there be some gratitude there? Anyway, they're not going to die without you. They'll send someone else, probably there's someone who would be glad to have that job."

"Yeah, maybe you're right. I mean, it was starting to wear me out."

My father recommended she start a business, "maybe something where you can fit in some of your other interests, not just nursing." The idea lingered, then languished, and after a few weeks I presumed it forgotten until, one afternoon when I was reading in my room, my father called me on his mobile phone. He'd had one since the late 1980s, and it sat pointlessly in his glove box, brought out only rarely, for show. The fees were eye-watering, so he reserved its use for tasks he knew he could dispatch in under a minute: calling the hotline for movie times or ringing me when he was outside my apartment, to save himself the inconvenience of leaving his car and climbing the steps to knock on my door. "You busy?" he asked.

"No."

"Come down, then, I've got something I want to show you. We can get some lunch on the way."

The drive took us from downtown past the housing projects and body shops over a wooded ridge flecked with motor lodges, a few once-elegant homes, and an always-empty restaurant called the Rib King, into a two-mile swath of drive-throughs and box stores around a dilapidated mall. The area had been suffocating since another, larger mall was built ten years before, and now many of the storefronts housed dubious outfits: for-profit trade schools, pawn shops, karate gyms, check cashers, massage parlors, fortune tellers. The bowling alley with its neon ten-pins, the endless fast-food franchises, and the soon-to-be-closed shops looked out over parking lots barely dotted with cars, and when they were visible past the pull blinds or the vinyl stickers in the windows advertising clearance pricing or zero-percent financing, the employees, leaning on counters or resting their elbows on tables, had uniform looks of despair.

At a traffic light, my father turned left and parked in one of three spaces behind a whitewashed building with a terrace precariously propped on four-by-fours. "What is this?" I asked.

"I'm about to show you." He took out two keys on a tempo-rary ring and opened a swinging glass door. Inside, the space was raw, with clots of spackle on the owl-gray Sheetrock and corrugated sheathing for the wires poking from the walls.

"What do you think?" my father asked.

"I don't know. I still don't know what it is."

"It's going to be a business," he said. "It'll be Karen's at first. Then we'll see where it goes. If it seems like something that has legs, I might leave the insurance game at some point and come on and try to make it grow."

"What kind of business?"

"We're gonna do a holistic health center. That stuff is getting big now. People don't trust doctors like they used to, they're starting to realize it's about lifestyle, about healthy living and not just fixing problems after they arise. People are scared of all this artificial stuff, they don't want to be just pumped full of drugs. We'll put a massage table here, we'll throw a sauna back there around that corner, those two rooms will be for counseling and meditation, and then we'll have like a desk here where we'll sell merchandise: natural oils and, uh, herbs."

"I didn't know you were into all that."

"Well, it's more her thing than mine, but I mean, yeah, I'm open-minded. If it makes people feel better, I'm all for it, and there's evidence that some of it works. I can tell you, in my field, you see things that would make your jaw drop: overprescription, unnecessary procedures, hell, they'll use a person like a guinea pig if they think they can bill for it. That doesn't mean if I get a staph infection I'm gonna ask some yogi to put a hot stone on it. But like, stress has a demonstrable effect on your blood pressure and on your sleep, and that can affect your cortisol levels, and there are all types of disorders tied to those kinds of hormonal imbalances. So do I think we should maybe step back and try and take a more balanced, less interventionist approach? Sure."

"But, like . . . does Karen know how to give massages?"

"Actually she does. She has a very intuitive sense of touch. But she doesn't have a license, not yet. We'll start off by hiring a therapist to come in a couple of days a week. We'll pay them an eighty-twenty split. Karen will start off really managing the place and trying to build up a list of clients for therapy. She was certified to do that before she moved down here, so it's just a matter of cutting through the red tape to get her credentials recognized. The long-term goal is for it to be a kind of learning center. Part of the business plan is these classes on mindfulness, emotional intelligence, neurolinguistic programming. If we can get ten or fifteen people coming down for that at thirty bucks per session, we could be looking at serious money."

"What's it going to be called?" I asked.

"CESID: The Center for Emotional, Spiritual, and Intellectual Development," my father said. An uncharismatic name, I thought: it sounded like a predatory insect. "One of the first things we'll to do to get it off the ground is print a newsletter, we got a mailing list of people to send it out to. Karen's been making calls to herbalists and stuff in town. Some are kind of weird—one was like an occult bookstore—but the response has been pretty positive, so who am I to judge? The idea is to try and partner with them, and then hopefully other businesses will hear about it and we can look into doing some cross-promotions."

"Cool," I said, unmoved but wishing to conceal my skepticism.

I asked if there was a restroom and was guided to the only finished space in the building, a closet with a vanity of pressboard and vinyl, an ovoid mirror, and a low toilet the color of custard. On the wall hung a small ring holding a phial of aromatic oil, with three sticks inside that might have been incense or pipe cleaners. When I closed the door behind me, I saw a gaudy poster in a plastic frame, the kind you see sometimes in dingy Indian restaurants. In an aureole of flowers, resembling caspia or sperm, a mauve baby draped in jewels like a rapper drew a porridge-like substance from an amphora with a club. The toilet hadn't recently been flushed, and the greasy sheen on the surface broke into topographical forms when I pissed inside it. I washed my hands, and my fingers went numb from the cold water. There were no paper towels, and the Kleenex tore off on my wet fingers when I dried them.

"All right then," my father said when I emerged. "You ready to head back?"

"Sure," I said, and skipped forward to open the door for him. As he walked past me, I watched his curious step, his heel barely touching the ground before his weight shifted to his toes and he arched his foot, as though in preparation for a sprint.

He reached behind the driver's seat to retrieve a paper sack with cardboard handles. "I got you something," he said. "Really it's from Karen and me, she wanted you to know it was her idea, too."

It was a book: *Are You Here? A Guide to Practical Mindfulness.*

"It's a little corny, some of it," my father said, "but it's not the Bible, just go through it and take it for what you can get out of it."

The author was a doctor of medicine and a professor in California who had studied yoga in Chennai with an allegedly renowned guru before returning to America, where he'd combined his spiritual instruction with the principles of experimental psychology. In the photograph on the back cover, he was seated in the lotus position in a lab coat and chinos, his thick furrows of dark hair streaked with gray.

Where are you now? the book began.

> Do you even know? Naturally few of us would be confused by such a question. And yet it implies an understanding of two mysterious things: who *you* are, and what it means for you to truly *be*. In my years in India, I came to understand that most of us are wrong on both counts: that the life we claim, the person we say we are, is a blend of fictions pulled from thin air and reactions to the prejudices and expectations of others. And being, for many people, is nothing more

than a series of routines society imposes on us to
make us forget what our existence is really about . . .

I flipped back to the front matter and looked at the chapter titles. They took the form of naive questions, heartening assertions, and imperious headings of a lone noun, often a neologism: after IS MINDFULNESS REAL SCIENCE? came YOUR BRAIN IS YOUR LAUNCHPAD, then TRUTH, NOWIFICATION, and HEARING / HERE-ING. The tone was anecdotal, with lots of "Aha"s and the occasional "Who'd a thunk it?" and the author derived spiritual wisdom from his own fitful failings, as in a four-page section devoted to his annoyance when his wife forgot to clean the hair trap in the shower, and instead of upbraiding her, he'd chosen to "manifest" the lessons he'd learned from the Buddha about the transitoriness of all things, including his resentments and his presumption that a well-ordered household would bring him happiness. By ignoring him, his wife had reminded him of the importance of patience, he concluded in A HAIR-BRAINED APPROACH TO ENLIGHTENMENT. "Even now, I find myself laughing when I see the water start to rise around the drain."

The following Sunday, Karen asked me about the book over dinner.

"So what did you think of Dr. Feehan-Ward?"

"Who?"

"The author of the book I gave you."

"Uh, yeah. He's interesting."

"I can still remember when I first found his work, I guess it was ten years ago," she said. "It was almost like fate. I was at the mall, I hadn't even been planning to go to the bookstore, and usually I wouldn't be caught dead in the self-help section. But I just happened to be wandering around aimlessly when it caught my eye. And right away, it spoke to me. I have always been interested in spirituality, you know, but with my ex, with my dad before him, it had to be their way, Christianity, Bible-thumping, Sunday school, church. And I did try. I really did. The gospels, you know, there were things I could take from that, love thy neighbor, I like the sound of that, throwing the money changers from the temple, but still. I didn't like the idea of people going to Hell and I didn't want to tell people it was wrong for them to get an abortion or decide who should have sex with who, I didn't see a spiritual basis for that, and that was all the Christians I knew seemed to care about. I was looking for peace, fellowship, not to condemn anybody else. And it was extra refreshing to see a doctor saying these things. I was working in health care so I was around lots of psychiatrists, but for them it was all here, take this drug, and I knew there had to be more to what-all I was going through than that. I bought this book at a tough time in my life, and it gave me hope in a way nothing else did. And I hope it works for you, too."

"I'm sure it will," I said, scratching little pebbles of boiled potato away from the skin with my fork.

"The truth is," my father said, "the scientific evidence for mindfulness just keeps piling up. I'm talking improvements in relationships, better immune function, reduced depression and anxiety . . . I even had a chat with our Health and Wellness director at work about implementing a mindfulness program for the employees, a lot of companies are doing it, they say it has major effects on productivity, your workers are less tired, they get along better . . . "

I felt the two of them observing me, and I doubted that I could suffuse the word "wow," the only one that occurred to me, with the least trace of authenticity. I nodded with what I hoped appeared a contemplative expression.

That night, when they took me back home, I opened the book to a page headed LET GO OF LETTING GO, which stressed the therapeutic and spiritual rewards of indifference. Too often, we approach mindfulness with the goal of finding enlightenment, the author wrote, but what was enlightenment, and why should it be any less hollow a goal than money, success, or whatever else society trained us to think that we desired? The point was not to achieve anything, not to do anything—the point was simply to *be*, the author said.

It struck me that simple being would be requisite not only for the attitudes the book recommended, but for those it deplored, and indeed for any attitude at all; I likewise sensed that there might be a discrepancy between the rejection of achievement and the positing of a "point"; but, regardless, I had never suffered malaise rooted in material or spiritual ambition, and had no difficulty letting go. My basic disposition was one of impassivity, which welled at times to all-encompassing aversion. Fear of obloquy, which Feehan-Ward chided as "giving in to the constructed aspect of your identity," was the only thing that kept me studying, or pretending to, or working or waking up or changing my clothes. Could the dividends of *mere being* really surpass those of clinging to the basic requirements of a relationship to one's family and one's world? I tried to imagine myself taking Dr. Feehan-Ward's lessons to heart, winding up a kind of holy man, dressed in rags and sleeping on the street, eating from trash cans, letting the filth gather under my nails because nothing mattered under the aspect of eternity. How long could it go on before I caught a disease, or my clothes started smelling of piss? As a program for existence, *mere being* wanted for inducements, and nothing I could imagine it offering looked likely to allay the sorrows of life, or to dampen the dread of death.

I flipped to a more practical chapter entitled HOW TO DO IT. The author warned:

> In our media-saturated age, most people feel a sudden alarm when deprived of stimulus. Don't be surprised, then, if you find it nearly impossible to stop the wheels from spinning: things you've heard on the radio or seen on TV will undoubtedly rise to the surface, like a low-level buzzing in the background. Find a quiet space, preferably somewhere dark and clean, where you won't be distracted. Don't try and stop the flow of thoughts—let them come, they will eventually empty out. When a memory arises, let it flow away. When anxiety about the future strikes, just say: That is not me. You are the thing that is here and now. Remember: You don't have to try and be what you already are.

I marked my page, lay back on the carpet, and closed my eyes, taking deep breaths. Immediately, my thoughts turned to sex. I remembered a seatmate from a seminar the year before, whom I'd never spoken to but had imagined courting with an almost disquieting degree of detail; I saw myself seducing, or failing to seduce, the hostess at work who used the word "passel" and rolled her eyes when I asked her what it meant, or meeting again with my second high school girlfriend, who cried just a bit but told me to keep going when we fucked in the room over the garage. All of this was beside the point, and so I pictured myself grasping these recollections physically and placing them in a lockable crate. Then I mused wearily on my upcoming exams. I was bored and, supposing this to be the mindful approach, I tried to understand my boredom, and to consider why boredom should bother me. When I could find no answer, I asked myself whether an answer was necessary, and what I would do were I to find one.

My roommate opened the front door, and I heard her boyfriend's trundling steps behind her. A football player from an agricultural college I suspected might not actually exist, he lived hours away and came to visit every few weeks. His suitcase hit the floor, and he told her not to forget to ask about getting him a gym pass in the morning.

"Come to my room," she said. "I think he's home."

Their presence, I told myself, would give me the opportunity to learn to turn away from distractions, and at each word they spoke, I reminded myself that everything they said was already part of the past, whereas I resided uniquely in the present. But they would not stop talking. To all appearances, their relationship was devoid of erotic sentiment, or any feeling at all, and rather resembled the tissue tropism that binds a host organism to its parasite. They talked disjointedly, with what psychologists call "poverty of affect," their conversations less like those of acquaintances or strangers than the dialogues from a first-year foreign language textbook. That night, for reasons I couldn't fathom, she asked him what sort of fruit he liked. His response was comprehensive, with frequent pauses from the strain:

"Lots. Bananas, pineapple, apples, of course, I mean there are lots of types of apples, I don't know if you count that as one fruit. Apricots, strawberries, raspberries, grapes . . . "

Everything you resent is already in the past, it is no longer there and was never a part of you, I thought.

"Blueberries, watermelon, coconut, grapefruit . . . "

Flustered, I sat back up, thinking the lotus position might help me concentrate.

"Did you know an eggplant is a fruit? I like those, too. Like eggplant Parmesan, you know. Oh, and, uh, what's it called, papaya, strawberries, limes . . . "

My heart pounded in my temples, his words gnawed at my nerves, but now I was thinking of fruits myself, and thinking surely to God he'd named all of them, I told myself it couldn't last much longer.

"Oh, what about figs? I didn't even think about those. Avocados, those are fruits, too. Pomegranate, kiwi . . . "

I grabbed the leather jacket lying thrown over the back of my futon and left, walking to the sports bar up the street to watch TV.

5

When I returned home at two in the morning, I found a green Post-It note on the threshold just past the screen door, its glue strip gray from pollen and dust. It was a message from my father in his barely decipherable cursive, stating he had come by in the hope of buying me dinner. He was sorry he had missed me, and would call in the morning. Doubtless my roommate, fearing his germs, hadn't opened when he knocked, and the wind had blown the note down during the night. The next morning, when the phone rang, I was too tired to go down and pick up. Since her boyfriend was with her, and her family called only on set days and times (she had no friends, so far as I could tell), she refused to answer, and shouted meekly, if such a thing is possible, "Phone's ringing. Probably for you." I ignored her, and once she left, I made a cup of her tea, hoping she would count the bags later and realize one was missing. Cup in hand, I walked out barefoot onto the splintering slats of the deck. The day was not pretty, but its drabness was agreeable, it held little promise but for that reason was undemanding; and the low light made the buildings and the trees lining the pavement, still damp from the previous night's rain, limpid and attractive to the eye.

It was ten in the morning, and even dawdling, I could easily make it to French. I probably wouldn't pass that semester, but thought I might yet try, and after dumping my cup in the sink, leaving the bag to stink and mildew, I put on a T-shirt and sneakers and walked the half mile to campus. Our lesson was on the use of the subjunctive in expressions of doubt, hope, and fear. My professor, a small woman of yellowing complexion whose disproportionate lower body made her look as though she was wearing a diaper, pointed at me after her introductory comments and asked:

"*As-tu peur des chiens?*"

"*Quoi?*"

"*J'ai dit, as-tu peur des chiens.*"

"*Non.*"

"*Pourquoi pas?*"

I could not answer, not only because I had no justification for not fearing dogs, but because I couldn't recall the subjunctive for any of the verbs that seemed pertinent to my reply. I tried to prevaricate with, "*Les chiens sont sympathiques.*" My professor explained for a second time the rationale behind the exercise and the form our answers should take, in French and briefly in English: "*J'ai peur que les chiens me mordent,*" I am afraid dogs might bite me. She posed me the question again, and I managed, with my mangled pronunciation, to say, "*J'aime bien les chiens.*" She explained the procedure again, with what I am sure she considered patience but what for me was a misplaced faith in the pedagogical utility of humiliation. I looked away, opening my hands in bewilderment, first at my activity partner to my left, then at the grainy plastic surface of the desk, covered with profanities in graphite and clues to exams past, until, after fifteen seconds of silent shame, she moved on to someone else.

I walked home afterward, and looking up from the road by the record store and a tailor's shop I had never seen open, with a dusty cotton torso and a sun-bleached suit in the display window, I saw my father leaning against the balustrade on the second floor of my building, his green overcoat thrown over one arm.

"Hey," he said to me after I'd climbed the stairs.

"Hey. What's up?"

"I missed you this morning on the phone."

"I didn't hear it. Probably I left it off the charger."

"Want to grab a coffee?"

"Sure."

We could have walked, but it was overcast, and he said he didn't want to get "caught out." As always, his car was immaculate inside, the dashboard and panels gleaming greasily and pregnant with the musk-and-rotting-citrus scent of Armor All. While he drove, he cursed the incompetence of everyone else on the road, including a squinting man in an early '70s Dodge Dart he called an *old goat*. After four blocks, he parked at a meter along the concrete median and told me to go in and order for him while he dug change out of the console.

The owner saluted me from behind the counter in one of those denim aprons with clasps that were just then becoming the accessory de rigueur for a certain theoretically more knowledgeable or dignified class of service worker. I ordered two coffees. "Just two regular coffees?" he said. Unfamiliar with the more intricate and costlier alternatives, and with no idea how to pronounce them, I said, "Yes, two regular coffees." My father walked in as I was sugaring mine, looked at the raised platform where we usually sat, and grimaced when he saw two girls there playing Pente. I met his eyes and pointed at another table flush with the wall. He nodded with what seemed like martial gravity.

"I'll tell you what," he said when we sat, "I'm fucking beat." He blew profusely across the rim of his cup and took the longest sip he could stand without burning himself.

"Late night?" I asked.

"Ha. That's one way of putting it."

"Work stuff?"

"I wish. Some bullshit with Karen. Probably best if I just keep it to myself. Probably not ideal for a parent to be airing their dirty laundry to their kid."

"I'm not really a kid," I said.

"I guess you're not, at that. Well, without getting into details, we haven't had the best time at home lately, right. There's things with the business, permits and shit, construction issues, what have you. I've been working my ass off, too, and uh, to be frank, I've probably let a few things slip. In our romantic life and all. So the other day I took off early, I said to myself, you know, I'm going to try and do it up today, something nice, something fancy, let her know I appreciate her. I go to the liquor store, I get a bottle of Taittinger, the good stuff, the one with the white label, *Comtes de Champagne*. I go to this little Mediterranean market, close to here, actually, and I get some olives and some prosciutto and feta and things like that. I knew she was going to be out for a while, so I went ahead and got dinner ready, I made a roast with this blue cheese sauce recipe I got from a guy I work with, a real gourmet type, just the sauce takes like two hours to make. So in short, I had everything set for a romantic evening. I dimmed the lights, put the candles around the house, classical music, all that. Long story short, we have our dinner and champagne, everything's nice, and I was like, I'm going to run a bath. She says OK, she's going to be there in a minute. I go ahead and start the water, and when it gets close to the top, I get in." Then he laughed in three breaths, staccato and guttural, like the grunt of a cormorant, and continued, "Well, this is kind of embarrassing, but right away I had to fart. And I mean, it would have been weird to get out sopping wet and walk over to the toilet, plus it was steamy as hell in there, I guess I thought the thing would dissipate. I don't really think it was that bad. So I'm lying there, I've got my eyes closed just waiting on her, she comes in and gets undressed, and all of a sudden she's like, 'What in God's name did you do?' I was too embarrassed to say anything but she just started screaming at me. 'You're disgusting,' she said, 'I can't even stand to be in here. How dare you,' she said. It was like she'd lost her goddamn mind. Honestly it's one of the strangest things I've ever seen."

I said, "But like . . . it's a bodily function. What did she expect you to do?"

"I don't know! I kept trying to tell her to relax, it's not a big deal and so forth. I was even like, look, I'll go get an air freshener or some incense or burn some candles. But she just wouldn't have it. Told me I'd ruined everything, I didn't respect her, and screams at me to get out of the tub, like I'd polluted it or something. And then she starts bawling her damn eyes out. Eventually I just said, this is ridiculous, I'm tired, my back hurts, you don't have to get in, but I'm going to stay in here as long as I want."

"So . . . ?"

"Then she just barges out of the room. So much for my romantic evening. I tried to stay in and soak for a while, but obviously I couldn't relax after that. I get out and towel off and start drying my hair, I was kind of thinking maybe I'd offer to go for a walk or something, but get this, she walks back in with her bathrobe and says to me: 'You need to go.'"

"Go?"

"Go. She said, 'You're disgusting, you didn't even have the decency to clean the tub.' I just tried to pretend it wasn't happening, like started to put my pajamas on and all, and she tears them out of my hand and shouts, 'Get the fuck out of here!' I said forget that, I'm not leaving my own goddamn house, but then Jesus, all that yelling and screaming, it just wouldn't stop, and after an hour or something I couldn't handle it anymore."

"What did you do?"

"You're not going to fucking believe this, but I slept in the doorway."

"What do you mean, the doorway?"

"Between the glassed-in door and the front door, in that little alcove with the umbrella stand and all. I just curled up there on the ground."

"You could have come over," I said.

"Well, I stopped by, but no one answered."

"Yeah, sorry. I didn't get your note till this morning. I was out late. I had to get out of the house. My roommate's boyfriend was over, he's a three-hundred-pound dimwit and his voice sounds like an alpenhorn. I was trying to get some peace in my room. I kept thinking he would finally shut up, but after a while I couldn't take it and I ended up going out. I'd have thought they'd respond if you knocked, but who knows, maybe they thought you were a burglar or a serial killer."

"It's fine. I could use a nap, but I survived."

"Have you talked to her today?"

"I left early, I went to a diner and got breakfast, I didn't want her to wake up before me and find me out there, who knows what she would have said. She did call, she left a message with my secretary, but I was in a meeting at the time and I wasn't ready to get back to her afterward."

"Man, if you still don't feel like it, you can come over. I'm off tonight. We could see a movie or something."

"Nah. Probably best just to face the music. I need a change of clothes anyway, I can't show up to the office like this tomorrow, and I'm sure as hell not going and buying a new outfit and toiletries because of this bullshit. In all likelihood she's gotten over it by now."

"All right," I said, and went to get a refill from one of the thermos pots lined up on a treadle sewing machine table—an antique touch, to give the place "character." When I returned, my father was tying the belt of his trench coat into an overhand knot rather than running it through the buckle. "I probably should be going," he said, hugged me, and left. I thought I might stay and read, but the shelves there, once stocked with dozens of books, had been plundered. Nothing was left but a Bible, a frayed stack of *National Geographic*, and *If There Be Thorns* by V. C. Andrews. I left my mug full on our table, walked home, grabbed my backpack, and went to the library with the intention of studying.

6

CESID opened two weeks later and my father invited me to the celebration.

He had painted the interior the drab yellow of ripening corn, and hung posters all over with backdrops of beaches, crags, or forests overlaid with inspirational slogans, some alleged to be Zen proverbs or ancient African wisdom: *When you seek it, you cannot find it*; *A man's character always dwells within him*; and the dubious *Choppy seas make good sailors.* In front of the counter was a card table covered with a patterned plastic sheet, where big bottles of flavored wine—Blackberry Merlot and Tropical Fruit Chardonnay—stood next to two stacks of Styrofoam cups. On the ground underneath it were two dozen cans of beer in crushed ice in a cooler. The crowd was sparse—men in suits, from my father's work, I guessed; a few women who must have worked with Karen at the home health care organization; several lost-looking people in corners drinking and looking down, presumably the local merchants with whom my father said CESID ought to *liaise.* Karen was in the main room, in front of three rows of folding plastic chairs, arranging a sign on a lectern with reflective letters that read WELCOME. My father waved to her, and she hurried over and gave him a kiss while he wrapped an arm around her waist and caressed the hollow between her ribs and hip. She patted his shoulder, pointed to where I stood, came over and hugged me, and thanked me for coming. Her labored exhalations, or her nerves, or her drinking, had made the blood rise in her face and neck, and her expression was at once animated and almost tragically apprehensive.

"You need help?" my father asked her, and she grabbed his fingers and tugged him away, and I returned to the counter to look through the pamphlets and business cards on display. She had hoped, when starting out, to form relationships with like-minded small businesses, but the few shops dealing in esoterica and holistic health were small and poorly located, and many seemed on the verge of bankruptcy. She would have to create interest rather than capitalize on it, my father had told her, and shouldn't let her prejudices blind her to opportunities. He was right, she had said, and had approached any organization or company that seemed a decent prospect. As a result, amid the expected circulars for vitamin shops and crystal healers were handbills for a shooting range, a Lebanese restaurant, a leather craftsman, and a portrait gallery. I poured myself a glass of red wine, which tasted of beet sugar and had a faintly mucosal texture. Ten minutes later, my father and Karen returned, he said, "I reckon this is everybody," and she stood on a chair in the waiting area, shouted, "Excuse me," and invited the group to the main room.

As people sat down, she walked behind the lectern, turned around and looked down into her own rosy cleavage, spanned by a necklace of variform polished stones. Then her eyes swept the room, and she coughed into her flattened hand.

"Everybody," she said, "I want to thank you for coming. Friends and, um, new friends alike. Opening CESID is definitely the craziest thing I've ever done, but seeing you all here makes me think maybe it will turn out all right." My father, standing, left shoulder leaned into the wall, clapped softly, and two or three people from the crowd followed suit.

"I guess to begin, I want to try and show people this isn't just the usual New Age nonsense you see on TV. We're not trying to push a religion, we're not trying to make people believe anything. I mean, I'm a nurse, I work in medicine, I believe in medicine, but there has to be a middle point. Look at how many people now are taking antidepressants or getting diagnosed with mental illness—aren't we at a place where we should examine the causes instead of just trying to treat the symptoms? For me, that's a lot of what mindfulness is about, and there are other things, less invasive therapies or better diet choices or supplements, that go along with that. Nobody here's a guru or a witch doctor. CESID is a space where we can gather and ask questions and learn, where we can think about the way we should be living and look at the way we're living now, and see what we can do to bring the two closer together. Now we've got a lot on the menu for you, a lot we're looking to expand into during the coming months. The first thing is going to be the mindfulness classes, we'll have those three times a week. Then we'll be bringing nutritionists in for seminars, we'll have a massage therapist on site, our goal is to be a one-stop holistic health resource, the only one in the area . . . "

She spoke for five more minutes, and when she finished, she was on the verge of tears. The crowd seemed to sense her anxiety, and applauded longer than was appropriate. When she stepped away, my father scurried to the lectern to remind people, "We've still got booze and munchies, and we're going to be here all night, so no need to scramble out," then walked up behind Karen and embraced her.

"Was I terrible?" she asked him.

"Don't be ridiculous," he said. "You were fantastic. The whole opening has been fantastic."

When my father asked me, some time later, if I was interested in attending a mindfulness class the following Thursday, I demurred, telling him I couldn't afford to miss work.

"Could you get off if I could make the money up to you?"

"I can't ask you to do that," I said.

"You're not asking *me* for anything," he replied. "I'm the one asking you for something."

"I guess I could try and switch my shift out."

"Here's the thing: the center's having a little bit of a rocky start. That doesn't worry me, it's just the way it goes, pretty much every business loses money the first year. But still, it's getting under Karen's skin. So I just think it might help her to see a few more people in the room, you know? And she likes you, she thinks you're intelligent, so you being there would maybe make her think, hey, you know, this isn't just some foolishness I've pulled out of my ass, normal people are interested in it, too."

"I'll see what I can do. I can't take your money, though."

"Bullshit," my father said, opening his wallet and removing four twenty-dollar bills.

"Is that enough?" he asked.

"I guess I just got a raise."

The Thursday came, gray and rainy, and I thought reluctantly of the evening ahead. I went downstairs, made coffee, and sat drinking it in the kitchen, to torment my roommate, knowing she wouldn't leave her room as long as I was there. When I finished, I blew my nose in the bathroom, swished water in my mouth, and walked upstairs. She hurried out in a huff, flushed my balled-up toilet tissue, and sprayed a misting of Lysol over all the things she thought I might have touched. It wasn't yet noon—I had nearly five hours before I'd need to catch the bus to CESID. I looked at my copy of *Are You Here?*, thinking of rehearsing one of the rituals prescribed therein to prepare for the concentration and seriousness the evening would demand. But the prospect was wearisome, and instead, after lying back down and listening for a while to the throaty coo of the pigeons bunched in the gutters, I took my umbrella and walked the half mile to a café, where I had a dry frittata for breakfast. There, in a tin rack painted a faded Prussian blue, were months' worth of back issues of tabloid magazines. Barely familiar with the celebrities they covered, and indifferent to the then-president's infidelity, which was the major news story of the day, I settled on a long account of a shooting at the offices of the Connecticut lottery. The murderer had been depressed over a change in his duties, and had taken a four-week leave for stress; in his absence, his former girlfriend had started seeing the worker who had replaced him. Colleagues reported he had changed while away, that on his return he was hostile and remote, "like talking to a stone." He resumed work for a week before coming in one morning armed and shooting four of his supervisors and then himself. His father stated that the killer had tried suicide multiple times, as recently as the previous year, with an overdose of pills; he'd found his son unconscious, dragged him out of bed, and driven him to the emergency room, where doctors had pumped his stomach and saved his life. "Maybe that was a mistake," the father was quoted as saying.

I put the magazine aside and watched the counter girl rinse out the pastel Fiestaware cups and set them upside down over a towel to dry. She was short, with a dyed blonde bob, narrow shoulders, small lips, and small hands; I had met her in high school at a friend's brother's party, but she'd either forgotten me or preferred to pretend she had. I sometimes sat at the bar when she was there, imagining I would mention this moment in our common past, find the occasion to make a charming remark, and ask if we might go out. The only attention she ever gave me was two terse smirks, forced and fleeting, one when I ordered, and one when I paid my tab.

I walked out and over to the glass and aluminum bus stop with its steel mesh bench and checked the schedule in the Lucite frame on the back wall. I looked across the street at the bank with the brick pillar out front supporting a rotating, cubical clock, and at the Irish restaurant Dirty Dick's, whose name, after a decade, still elicited giggles from the city's residents. As the bus approached, a white rectangle with the letters MARTS painted in red on its side, I remembered the joke wealthier white kids from high school used to make about the initials of the not-at-all-rapid Metropolitan Area Rapid Transit System: Moving Africans and Rednecks Through the Southeast. My fare was a dollar thirty.

The floor of the bus was grooved pink plastic, with white marbling, like a cut of bacon; the only passengers were a man in his fifties in a Carhartt jacket, paint-spattered jeans, and work boots, and a wizened woman buried in her feather coat, her shopping cart stuffed with paper bags. As the crow flew, CESID was six miles from the bus stop, and the fastest route by car was nine; but because the bus lines were few, each took a tortuous path, and we would sweep out far beyond downtown, braking at the shopping center past the hydroelectric dam, at the community college, and at assorted desolate public agencies along a little-trafficked turnpike before reaching the stop where the driver would let me off. I closed my eyes and felt the bus tossing like a ship, opening them every five minutes to get a sense of how far we'd gone.

To the north, a diffuse apricot glow, smudged and sallow at the edges, hinted at the end of the rain, which had plunked regularly against the windows, forming rills, throughout the trip, until the passing trucks raised up sheets of spray that flattened them. By the time I got out, it had thinned to a drizzle, and I didn't bother to open my umbrella. The sidewalk was intermittent between the bus stop and CESID, making one wonder who the city planners thought would begin their itinerary a quarter mile past a grocery store and reach their destination at a culvert; where the pavement ended, I had to walk a thin path trod by vagrants, littered with beer bottles and takeout containers, occasionally protected by a guardrail. Mud clung to my shoes; I couldn't wear them into the record store or a diner along the way, so I kept walking, hoping Karen had shown up early and I could clean them in the sink.

Ahead I saw a sign: a grand piano of black and white plastic, the keys serving as teeth, with two eerie eyes on the narrow part of the lid. This was the music store on the floor above the mindfulness center, on the side that faced the street. I turned left, walked around back, and saw Karen in a patchwork jacket

61

behind her car, pulling alternately on two sides of a cardboard box, trying to ease it out of the trunk.

"Want a hand?" I asked.

"Oh, Jesus, yes."

"What is it?"

"It's a goddamn fountain. I just got it at Walmart. I thought it would help set the mood in the mindfulness room. It didn't cost much, and they said it would be easy to set up, but when this nice young man brought it out for me, I didn't think to ask him how I'd get it out of the car."

We pulled it halfway across the lip of the trunk, and I squatted down, holding it steady so it wouldn't slip out and fall to the ground. Karen eased it back and forth until it rested on my knees, then we set down one corner, I pushed my way out from under it, and it fell flat with a short series of clunks in its interior. She stood back and stared at it, hands pressed into the small of her back, and said, "Let's just push the damn thing," which we did, scraping it across the asphalt till we reached the door. To get it inside, we tipped it over the doorjamb and laid it out horizontally.

"Give me just a second," I said.

I stopped on the threshold, took off my shoes, and pounded them on the pavement while Karen slit the tape on the seams of the box top with a key. Dirt was wedged into the treads, so I took them to the bathroom to run water over the soles and pick at them with a ballpoint pen. It fell out in rectilinear strips and Vs that dissolved slowly at the edge of the drain. Soon I heard a series of exclamations: a man's staccato laughter, deeper and hoarser than my father's, an *Oh my God!* from Karen, a *You like that, don't you?* from the man. When I went out to look for a towel, I saw a short, gray-haired figure with a mealy scarlet face, gelid blue eyes, and disconcertingly white teeth. "Hey there," he said when he saw me, charging forward, hand flat and brandished like a weapon, "I'm Kent, Kent Minter, here for the mindfulness class. You?"

"He's our neighbor," Karen said while he shook my hand up and down as though hoping to dislocate my elbow. He was dressed in a red muumuu printed with a coconut pattern.

"What on earth are you doing in that thing?" she asked.

"Come on, now, Karen, don't you find it debonair? I thought the dress code called for something spiritual-looking. Did I read the invitation wrong? Anyway, you seemed all tense when you were up here talking the other day. I thought it was worth it to try and give you a laugh."

"Well, you've certainly done that."

"What's this we've got over here?"

"It's supposed to be a fountain. Too bad we can't manage to get it out of the box."

"Well, here now, step aside and let's me and this young man give it a try, I'll bet between us we can get it up and running in no time."

Kent Minter grabbed my shoulder and guided me over. There were three parts: a ceramic bowl painted to resemble slate; an egg-shaped vessel with a rough outer surface and a hollow niche illuminated by a battery-powered light; and a muscular, serene Buddha, glimmering gold and draped in a pale sheet, to be set inside the egg, so the water would cascade before his eyes. While I was tearing away a piece of the cardboard to leave my shoes on by the door, Kent carried the first piece into the other room. I followed him, but he told me to wait while he consulted the manual, and after exclaiming "piece of cake," he assembled it in minutes, plugging it in and arranging the Buddha once egg and bowl were fitted together. Karen fetched water from the bathroom, and when she turned the contraption on, it made a dull hum, quickly followed by a trickling sound like urine splashing in a puddle.

"Oh, that's perfect!" Karen said.

"It is *so* calming," Kent Minter replied.

Fifteen minutes later, three more people arrived and presented themselves, and once it was clear no one else would show, the five of us sat in a circle, with the lights dimmed, in the room with the fountain, while Karen stayed standing, an open book in her hand.

"Well, thanks for coming, everyone. There's not too many of us," she said, "but that's probably for the best, starting off. This is a new thing for me, I'm sure it's new for you, so it'll be a learning experience for all of us."

She began by entreating us to relax, bow our heads, and close our eyes. We took deep, rhythmic breaths as Karen counted: *Inhale, one, two, three, four, exhale, one, two, three, four.* I looked up at the other students: there was an obese man with a beard, a thin, older woman with dark skin and hair bleached to a horrible, exhausted orange color, a girl around my age with scattered violet welts—hives, mosquito bites, or track marks—on her forearms. "Feel the floor, the weight of your body on the floor, let your limbs, your head relax. We're going to start by just noticing our breath." The obese man seemed to suffer from rhinitis: each of his breaths began with an audible pop, followed by a grunt and swallow.

"Just let your breath anchor you," Karen continued. "Now we'll start into the deep meditation. While you sit there, you'll notice sensations, but also emotions, they'll rise up, don't try to ignore them or control them. You don't have to do anything, just be in the present, experience the feeling of it, but don't try to hold onto it or run from it. You may notice a tension in your chest or shoulders, you may think about your worries or fears, you may remember some obligation you have coming up, but all of that, you can just let it go. Whatever happens, just keep coming back to your breath, that's your rock, and keep letting yourself relax more and more."

I was falling asleep. My head dipped and jerked up, and I opened my eyes and saw the group intent in its reverie. When Karen glanced over, I closed them again and listened to her monologue. "Today, we want to talk about breaking free from our fears, which hold us back from experiencing our lives as they are. Whether it's a fear in your marriage, at your job, whether you're afraid you might never do the thing you've always wanted to do, I want you to stop for a moment and let that burden go. Just be here, just realize there's nothing you can do about it. Realize your fear is your heart opening toward what it loves, and that in yourself, you already possess the thing you love, here and now, you are already with it." I had been preoccupied with no such specific anxiety or longing to speak of, but now these came crowding in: I thought of my ex-girlfriend, Fox, whom I yearned to touch again; of the possibility that I might never finish school, or that I would finish it without arriving at any sense of what to do after. I tried to follow Karen's words, to see myself letting go, to envision these abstractions as physical things I could squeeze in my hand, cherish for a moment, and then release; but my concentration was interrupted by the digestive noises of her pupils, now high-pitched, now grave, now percussive when the air gurgled up through a gullet. "For fuck's sake," I heard Karen murmur. "Can people please remember to have breakfast before class?"

7

My father called a few days later to ask how the session had gone, and to see whether I was up for attending another. "I wouldn't say no right out," I said, "it was really relaxing. But it's not the best time of year for me. Things are getting crazy at work, they've been calling me in on my off-days, and I've got finals coming up, too." With the cliché, *you know, studies have shown*, he claimed mindfulness might help with my grades, but soon he saw there was no point. Dr. Feehan-Ward had failed to persuade me. I had not managed to understand what distinguished the feeling of meditation from that of sitting anywhere, uninspired and bored, and letting my mind wander, as I had already been doing for most of each day of my life.

On occasion, I asked my father his thoughts about the business. If his mood was good, he would tell me, "I think we're making progress"; if bad, he would reflect, "Doing things on your own is a struggle." It was a small town, the residents were conservative, it was hard to make headway among people who still believed Jesus had roamed the earth alongside the dinosaurs. "We actually get people asking us if mindfulness and devil worship are the same thing." Karen took her work seriously and expected her students to do the same, but their attendance was irregular, and their questions revealed how few of them were keeping up with the reading. Some of them smelled bad, and that made it difficult to focus on the mantras. There was one old man who couldn't get through a forty-minute class without leaving the room to pee. "Half the time it's no better than looking after children," she told my father.

My father began to call off our Sunday dinners. Sometimes he said Karen had a migraine, other times that he had taken home too much work. I didn't mind the respite; in the four months since they had moved in, we had said all we had to say to each other, and more and more, the conversations, such as they were, had become forced.

For the holidays, Karen asked if they could visit her family, whom she hadn't seen since moving south. My father said yes, and invited me along. I didn't care to go, but had no plausible motive for refusing. I had already told him my work was closed for the week of Christmas, and winter break had started ten days before. "It'll be fun," my father said, improbably. "Kansas City, it's a cool town, it's not too long a trip, we'll break it up into two days. I'll do the driving myself, I really don't mind. I went to the rental car place and checked out this conversion van, man, this thing has all the bells and whistles—TV, VCR, and it can easily sleep three. We'll stop at a campground on the way up, maybe go for a hike in the woods."

The day before we left, my father called to say he was at Walmart and ask if I'd like any "goodies" for the way up. I said I didn't care. I was in a rush; I'd slept through to the afternoon and had to shower and dress for work. Winter was the party season. All the big companies had banquets, and when they ended, cliques of coworkers would leave their long tables for the bar, where they would drink themselves blind, sing and dance, take cocaine in the bathroom, sometimes vomit, sometimes fuck in the alley next to the dumpsters. The whole week, whenever I took out the trash or went to the dining room to mop up a spill, I would see people I'd known in high school who were now about to graduate and had internships in real estate or engineering, professions as foreign and exotic for me as those of bounty hunter or deep-sea explorer; already at twenty, their hair was thinning, their shoulders too narrow, their midriffs swollen against the golf shirts tucked into their pants behind their braided leather belts. "How you doing?" we asked each other, and always responded, "Same old, same old." It wasn't pleasant, and I was relieved when it ended.

The back door lay between two rows of folded cardboard boxes stacked with black bags of trash, with fat and oil pooling in the cracks in the asphalt underneath. The door was propped open with a wooden wedge in the hinges. I turned the corner by the stainless-steel prep tables and entered the dish room. Wayne, the "head dishwasher," a post of his own invention, was running a squeegee through tomato-tinted water and channeling it into a grated insert in the sink. Tinnily reverberating from a cheap portable stereo was the same 8Ball & MJG tape he'd had in for the past six months:

These hoes think I slang birds 'cause I'm living comfortable,
Fool I had to struggle 'cause my father ain't Cliff Huxtable

He pulled a lever on the side of the dish machine; the guillotine door slid up and gusted steam puffs; and he jerked out a basket of flatware.

"Sort dat," he said.

He scrubbed food off the plates, sprayed them with a hose, and pushed them into the machine; when they emerged, wet and so hot they scalded my fingertips, I'd stack them and take them to the line. While the machine cycled through the next batch, I scrubbed pans and sorted silver. I hated this arrangement, yet it was somehow immutable. Every hour, Wayne sat down in the crumbling chair between the men's and women's employee restrooms and smoked his cigarette idly before walking to the servers' alley, melting a half-cup of sugar with hot water from the coffee machine, and stirring it into his iced tea. The pans proliferated, turning the soap in the basins coral pink, until around eight, when Wayne snorted in disappointment and said, "Damn, man." He reached deep in one sink, retrieved a tuft of steel wool, and scrubbed the pans free of crust with almost superhuman briskness, sending bits of congealed cheese dip and burnt brown peppers flying.

"Keep them pans up now," he called out over his shoulder. "They a fuck you up you don't stay on top of them." He had given me the same advice almost nightly for months.

At nine a bloated body tottered in with a clownish limp, sucking breath through disordered, greenish teeth. He wiped his knurled brow, filled a plastic cup with soda, and hobbled into the dish room. When he saw me, he held out a chubby mitt that almost swallowed my hand whole. "Hiya," he said, his voice high as a newborn baby's.

"'Bout time, you fat fucker," said Wayne. "You was 'spose to be here at six."

"Couldn't get a ride," the man warbled.

"You ain't gone need no ride you pull this shit again," Wayne said. "I'll beat you ass so bad they fix you up wit' one of dem mechanical wheelchairs wit' the joystick and shit."

The man rolled his eyes as Wayne bundled his apron and dropped it into a cloth sack stretched over a metal frame. "Ah'm Jerry," he said.

"Oh, shit," said Joe, one of the line cooks. "You ain't met Jerry? Boy, you can go 'head kick your feet up, Jerry, he a speed demon, he a run that dish room by hisself."

"Shut up," Jerry said.

"You shut up, you old big-head, biscuit-eatin' mothafucka. He say he do repair work on the side, right, like he got a business. He look like a businessman to you? He come up in here the other day tryin' a sell me a laser disc player."

"So?" the baby's voice asked.

"Man, ain't nobody even know what a goddamn laser disc is!"

"It's high-tech."

"Don't buy no shit from Jerry," Joe said, pointed at me, and stepped away.

The banquets brought lulls and rushes; for half an hour there was nothing to do, then the busboys would come in with plates stacked twenty high. Since he was working the tail end of Wayne's shift, Jerry had presumed he would take his place in the pit; unlike Wayne, he showed no sympathy when I began to fall behind. Later, after I'd washed the exhaust hoods, the manager told me to have a smoke. I was quitting, I said, and he responded, "Then have a Coke or a coffee, what the fuck do I care, just go sit down for a little bit, let Jerry pull the load." I walked around the corner and leaned against the wall. Blunt aches slithered through my back and knees. Two Mexican women filled buckets from a spigot and dashed them across the floor of the pantry, setting afloat scraps of ham and the furred caps of onions that had been kicked under the ice machines. One pushed the refuse toward a drain with a squeegee; the other followed behind her with a mop.

When ten struck, the kitchen pulled their pans from the refrigerated cabinets and dumped them on the dish counter along with the grease traps and the scorched burners. I worked at them with a scouring pad and a bench scraper for the clingy bits until the soggy skin on my fingertips started rubbing off. When I caught a cook's eye, I asked, "Where the fuck is Jerry?" He jerked his head toward the door leading outside.

I walked out and found him sitting in a chair he had dragged out from the dining room, his work shirt over his knee and a white T-shirt pulled over one arm and partway down the crown of his head. His body was pristine like an egg, of an immutable porcelain white untarnished by hair, rolls, or freckles. His head pressed at the shirt's neckline, pushed up, then burst through with a dismal whimper. After working through his other arm, he drew a deep breath and looked at the ground.

"You all right?" I asked.

"All right? Shit, ah got the gout, high blood pressure, emphysema . . . Bad circulation in my feet. Head hurts like a sonofabitch 'cause ah got this toothache back there in the back, ah just lost one the other day. Bit into a piece of that Parmesan cheese they got back there and it come clean out by the root. Ah can still feel that all the way down into my neck. Doctor said ah'm not supposed to be standing up this long, you know, ah got a couple of bad discs in my back, it's killin' me. You name it, man, ah got diabetes, asthma. My old man croaked when he was thirty-six. Ah'm thirty-two now. Don't give me a lot of time, does it?"

He gazed up at me, his eyes green in yellow whites tinseled with burst blood vessels, wondering perhaps what I'd made of this presumably rehearsed inventory of misfortunes. I was unprepared to agree that he likely would die soon, so I mumbled about healthy diets and no one knowing when his day would come, then said, "Everything's basically done in there, you just gotta wipe the counters and take apart the machine. I'm punching out, I'm going out of town tomorrow."

"OK," he cooed dejectedly.

I got drunk on the way home, and when my father called from his cellphone the next morning to say he was parked in front of my building, my mouth was dry and pasty and a sound like amplifier feedback drilled into my head at the temples.

I said, "Give me a sec. I had a late night at work. I'm still not totally together."

"That's fine," he said. "I'm coming up, I'll give you a hand."

I said there was no need, but he insisted, and hung up before I could refuse again. I stood, grabbed clothing at random from the floor and my closet, plus a book and my toothbrush, swished a gulp of mouthwash and spit it into the tub, and walked downstairs, stopping once and clutching the banister to keep from throwing up.

"I'm good, I'm ready," I said when I heard my father's knocks on the door, but when I opened, his neck pitched forward like a pigeon's and his red nose, shiny with skin oil, wedged past the doorjamb. He brought a raised finger to his lips, then took off his glasses and ran the thumb of his opposite hand over the swells of his eyelids.

"Everything all right?" I asked.

"Yeah, yeah," he whispered. "I just want to get you ready for the trip."

"How so?" I said.

"Ah, just some things about Karen. Nothing major. She's not been having the best few weeks."

"She alright?"

"Yeah, yeah. It's just that, uh, CESID, you know, it's not doing too well. And I think she's a little homesick, or stir-crazy, or what have you. She started seeing a therapist, he's got her on some meds. I do think that'll help, but they take time to kick in. So really I just wanted to come up and tell you she's not feeling that good today, and you shouldn't let it put you off if she's not her usual jovial self. She'll snap out of it, but maybe we'll give her a little space for the next couple hours."

"OK."

When I walked downstairs, I saw Karen in the passenger seat in a satin dress and oversized sunglasses like the ones people wear to funerals. I slid open the side door, got into the backseat, and said, "Let me know if you'd rather sit back here. I don't mind riding in the front."

"No, I'm fine."

"I didn't get the chance to ask how you were doing. You look a little under the weather," my father said.

"I'm tired from work. We've been busy," I said.

"Well hey, feel free to stretch out and take a nap."

The van had rows of plastic-coated track lights along the edges of the floor and roof. I lay down across the seats, but whenever we changed lanes, I got queasy. Traffic was light, and my father topped seventy as he drove beneath the overpass onto the freeway.

The day was hot, and the front windows were cracked, letting a breeze circulate through the van. The fresh air did me good, and my nausea subsided. No one seemed inclined to speak. I took out my book, Boris Pilnyak's *The Naked Year*, and read about Ivan, the punctilious stationer, who would show up at his shop early to harangue the apprentices: *Do not say give, but present, do not say bargain, but discuss.* Soon we were out of the city, passing through forests that grew in lushness, losing, little by little, the obvious print of human hands, but of course this was a deception; when I remarked on how nice it was to see the hardwoods instead of the eucalyptus that covered the ridges where we lived, my father told me the trees had been planted in the thirties to prevent erosion. He said he remembered when his father had taken him there as a boy, to admire the rock formations and waterfalls and to fish in the man-made lake. "In those days," he said, "not a one of them was more than twenty feet tall."

Karen grew animated just before night fell, when the campsite was a half hour away. "Well, this is going to be great," she said, her first words since we'd gotten on the road. She turned back to me and told me she had bought marshmallows to roast over the fire. "Just like summer camp," she said. "We can sit around and tell ghost stories."

"I hardly think we'll be building a fire," my father said.

"Oh, you're such a wet blanket," she said.

A wooden sign in garish colors marked the exit for the campsite. Past a welcome center with a host of flagpoles in the front and souvenirs twinkling through the windows stood a handful of cabins stained a ghastly orange and four rows of lots branching off two gravel roads. My father stopped and went inside to ask for our number, then turned right, parking between an Airstream trailer and a grill where a group of bikers was cooking hot dogs.

"Yay!" Karen said when my father took the key from the ignition.

While I helped my father remove the seats, turning them and folding them out into beds, his wife dug through her rolling suitcase, setting aside her iron, hair dryer, and shoes, until she found a strand of lights with plastic casings in the form of zoo animals, which she strung along one side of the van. I saw her through the window, eyes wide with concentration, the tip of her tongue poking from one corner of her lips.

"What's she doing?" I asked my father.

"Ah, it's just some silly lights she bought. She said if we had to stop and stay the night, we might as well make it festive."

He took a long time adjusting the fitted sheet, and seemed not to want to look up. When Karen opened the passenger door to plug the adapter into the cigarette lighter, my father told her, "No more than thirty minutes. We talked about this, I told you, you could run down the battery."

"Oh, for God's sake, just try and have a bit of fun," she replied.

We put on jackets, and my father walked to the welcome center with a plastic bucket to get ice for his beers.

"Let's watch a movie," his wife said when he returned.

"Ah, shit," my father said.

"What?" I asked.

"I had a whole bag of tapes set aside to bring, and I left the goddamn thing by the door."

"Perfect," Karen replied.

I said, "Maybe there's something in the van somewhere."

I looked in the glove compartment and underneath the seat, but all I found was *House Party 3*, starring the rappers Kid 'n Play. My father announced that he hated rap, and sighed through the opening credits. Karen punched him on the shoulder, said, "Come on, old man, get with the times," and like me, tried to feign enthusiasm. But even she was soon exasperated. All of us could see which moments were meant to be humorous: the actors even paused, giving time for the audience to think a gag through, and nearly every joke was a pun referring to the line that preceded it—yet to laugh at them was impossible, and even the thought that anyone had ever done so caused dejection. We held out until a dinner scene with a burnt suckling pig on the table, which Bernie Mac stabbed at while a family sneered at him in a hollow send-up of aristocratic manners. When he shouted his famous phrase, "Now I got to cut you," which I'd heard repeated ad nauseam by all my coworkers the year before, Karen pressed stop, my father said, "Finally," and we agreed to go to sleep.

I was still hung over, and the sensation of falling kept jarring me awake. Outside, two drunks were arguing about something, a kind of motor, to all appearances; their discussion consisted mainly of yelling the words "bullshit" and "bullshit yourself" in turn. I drifted off, and woke later to my father's own cursing.

"Goddammit! Son of a fucking bitch!"

I sat up and looked out the window, but when I didn't see him, I fell back to sleep, thinking he had gone out barefoot and stepped on a can or a shard of glass. I dreamed I'd been sent back to high school to retake a class I'd forgotten I'd failed, and was struggling to make friends with students years younger than myself. Then I heard Karen shouting, and as soon as I woke,

I started retching as a fetor saturated the van, a smell of burnt rubber mingled with hot garbage.

"What is that?" Karen shouted.

"I went out for a piss and got sprayed by a goddamn skunk," my father said.

"Well, go wash it off!" his wife shouted.

"I did, damn it, I've been hosing myself off for forty-five minutes!"

"Christ, close the door, it's awful," his wife said.

"What do you mean, close the door? You want me to stay out here all night and sleep on the fucking ground? It's 3 a.m. and I've got to drive another four hours in the morning."

"Well, I don't know what to tell you, but you better do something, there's no way you're coming back in here."

"For real? You don't even care? The water from that hose is ice cold, my toes feel like they're frostbitten."

"You're right, I don't care! You're a big boy, figure something out. I can't talk about it anymore, if I smell that for another second I'm going to puke."

She pulled the door closed. I saw my father's face, bewildered, through the window. He rapped two or three times on the glass with his knuckles until his wife swore and opened back up. He couldn't just stand there, he pleaded, he needed to talk to her and figure out what they should do. She put on a pair of slippers, threw a blanket over her shoulders, and went outside. They walked up the road, fifteen feet between them. I couldn't hear what she was saying, only his replies. "Let's just go to a hotel," he said; then, "I don't care"; then, "Fine, I'll sleep in the goddamn van."

As they walked back, she said she didn't know if she could ride with him.

"Hold the blanket in front of your nose," he said.

When my father returned, he opened the back door and asked if I'd heard what they were talking about.

"More or less."

"Yeah, I'm sure you smelled it, too."

He threw his suitcase, which he had taken to the welcome center, back inside. He offered to help fold the seats into position, but then said, "Probably better if I don't."

"I think we're good," I told him once everything was arranged.

He got in, started the engine, and looked back pitifully at his wife, who was hiding her face in a bundle of bedclothes. After a moment she peeked out, furrowed her brows, and said, "Oh please. Can we just get out of here?"

As my father reversed, we heard a crunch, then a clatter like trotting horseshoes.

"My lights!" Karen said.

"Fuck your lights. We'll get some new ones later," my father said.

The stench on him did not diminish, but revealed new layers as we grew accustomed to the more patently repulsive notes, in a kind of inversion of the acquired pleasure connoisseurs claim to find in Scotch or cigars. Sulfur gave way to putrefaction, putrefaction to intestinal gas, but tinged with something musky and sweet, like opium gum. My father rolled down the front windows, but the cold air rushing in only blew the rot back in our faces. I closed my eyes and tried to concentrate on breathing through my mouth, but the odor clung to my palate and the inside of my cheeks. My father's wife retched and clamored: "What are we going to do?"

We stopped at a motel, a squat building that paired the lowest architectural standards with the elaborate and pointless conceit of a turreted tower clad in cultured stone. My father was ashamed to go inside, and asked Karen to pay for the room; she didn't want to, because she was in her nightgown and her hair was pinned up. Finally he took out his cellphone, called the number listed on the door, read out his credit card information to the attendant, and asked me to go in to retrieve the key. He and his wife argued about who should stay in the room. After his travails, my father must have looked forward to lying in a bed alone, watching television, and letting his frustration subside, but his wife said it only made sense for him stay in the van, so he could drive to the nearest town when the sun rose to buy peroxide and baking soda to get rid of the scent. The room he rented had two single beds; it was assumed I would take one. From solidarity with ignominy, I offered to stay in the van and keep him company. He lowered his eyelids, pursed his lips, gave me a wry "Please," and pointed at the door.

The next morning, he spent an hour cleaning himself while his wife and I ate pancakes and drank coffee at one of three card tables in a corner of the motel office. He threw his pajamas and shoes into the dumpster. By nine, we were back on the road. Karen's good humor had returned, and my father's as well: from the backseat, I could see their hands slacken by their hips, their fingers stiffen and bow, graze at the tips, and then come together in a clasp. Karen turned the radio up loud and began to sing.

Three hours later, a huge hotel came into view, and behind it, the nine or ten most prominent towers of the Kansas City skyline. My father asked Karen to call her family and let them know we were near. After a few minutes' chitchat, cut short by my father's riffling imaginary dollars in his right hand, she said she needed to hang up. Her family asked if she was hungry, and when she said yes, told her to meet them at a restaurant for a late lunch.

"Do you like barbecue?" Karen asked me. "Well, you're going to love this place."

Her parents, her brother, and her nephew were there to meet us. The restaurant was large and scantily adorned, with Formica tables, metal chairs, and yellowed photos of bygone celebrities on the wall. Karen's father was decrepit and wore a dark cap embroidered with a warship. My father made a point of shaking his hand and remarking on the type of vessel depicted, asking whether it had been built in the New York or Philadelphia ship-yard. I had never known my father to show interest in nautical matters, and assumed he had furnished himself with this bit of patriotic trivia for the occasion. It failed to achieve the desired effect, I think, as none of us could understand the old man's opaquely mumbled responses.

The food was viscid, sweet, and salty, and I had to wipe my hands and mouth after each bite. Karen's parents spoke little, and once we'd run through the niceties, talk turned to politics. Karen's brother trotted out timeworn clichés about gun owner-ship and welfare. My father tried vainly to combat them, citing statistics about accidental gun deaths and decrying anti-welfare sentiment as covert racism, but when the veins swelled beneath the freckled skin of his neck, his wife, anxious or weary of her brother's routine, struck the table, silencing them both. She smiled and said, "I seem to remember when we grew up they taught us not to talk politics at the dinner table."

Her nephew, a police officer a few years my senior, asked if I felt like going out that night. I said no, that I wanted to catch up on sleep. This opened the floor for Karen to recount my father's misadventure with the skunk. She laughed throughout the telling, and tears glimmered like small jewels in the outer corners of her eyes. My father stared into his plate, and then away, toward the service counter, biting his lower lip to keep from frowning.

Later that week, at the art museum, we saw a reproduction of Rodin's *The Thinker*, verdigris and perplexed, on a pink granite plinth with a pigeon posted on his head, but we couldn't enter, as the museum was closed for the holidays. We drove by a baseball stadium, also closed, and had lunch and coffee in what Karen's family described as a "quirky area" with "funky boutiques and shops." On Christmas Eve, we exchanged gifts. My father had bought several mounted plastic fish that sang and flapped their tails at the push of a button; they were thought very funny, and it was hours before their tinny jingle subsided. I received several low-denomination gift certificates to chain stores and restaurants, all tendered with the excuse, "We didn't really know you, so . . . "

When the festivities were over, and the older people were drinking mulled wine and coffee with whiskey, Karen's nephew invited me out once more, whispering to me that he and his friends were going to a strip club. When I told him no thanks, that I would stay in and read, he touched together his thumbs and index fingers and mouthed the word *vagina*. "I'm going to go on to that church thing I was telling y'all about," he said to his family.

I stayed up after everyone had gone to bed, first reading, then watching B movies on TV. Thinking it might relax me, I took a shower. The water was hot, and the steam fogged over the sliding glass panels. I masturbated, and after coming, stepped out and found my father's wife standing next to the sink. I froze, then reached blindly for the pink towel hanging on the rack.

"Jesus, I'm sorry," she said, "I just woke up and had to pee. I didn't even realize anyone was in here."

She started to leave, then turned and whispered:

"Don't say anything to your father."

8

A few weeks later, my father rattled my storm door.

It was drizzling. Runoff was audible, plinking over the eaves, roars echoing over the smoke-pale clouds, and the wind whistled shrill through the branches of the trees lining the road. My father's green raincoat was mottled with silver drops. He held a plastic bag in his hand. The red and blue label of a six-pack of beer showed through it. His head was hanging, his shoulders slack, and he was puckering and dilating his thin, purple lips.

"Can I come in?" he asked.

When I said yes, he wrapped both hands around the knob, as though handling something sordid or fragile. When he had shut it behind him, he looked back and stroked a tassel of pink glass beads a friend had hung under the peephole when I first moved in, to put some color into my life, she said.

My roommate hadn't come back after the holidays. Her parents had called one day to say she was sick, that they would continue paying her half of the rent but weren't sure when she would return. From vague ascetic inclinations, I had since decorated the apartment in what I took to be a Japanese style. Spare surroundings, I believed, would help impart the grave disposition necessary to finish my studies and arrive at a more adult conduct of life. In fact, this caprice inspired nothing more than lethargy and the desire to leave no sooner than I'd awakened, but once it was done, I didn't have the money to change it back. There was a futon on the floor, a low, lacquered coffee table, a rug embroidered with acacia fronds, and a pile of pillows. My father swept his eyes over the absence of furnishings, unsure of where to sit.

"You can just sit on the futon if you want," I said.

His eye sockets, and the ridges where they met his cheekbones, were wrinkled and yellowish, and the pale pink of his eye-whites was overrun with red rays. He blinked incessantly. He set the plastic bag in the middle of the table, knelt, and slid his legs underneath; then, with a kind of spasmodic flop, raising himself on one arm, he wedged a cushion under his buttocks. His coat gaped open, revealing a woolly plaid interior. The few hairs, chalk-white and walnut, that composed his spare combover, were crooked and disarrayed, as if by shock. He sighed and took a beer out of the bag.

"You want one of these?" he asked, trying to smile, but bereft of all aptitude for jollity.

"No thanks, I'm fine. I still haven't had my coffee."

"It's pretty pathetic, really. I mean, how mature is that, turning to alcohol to solve your problems? I basically don't drink anymore, except for last night, because I'm trying to lose a couple pounds, but today I just didn't know what else to do."

"What happened?"

"Ah . . . I don't know. It's just payback, really. Bad karma, I guess." He continued to mumble and prevaricate, letting a squinted-through exhalation, a crack of the knuckles, or a tug at his hooked mustache tips stand in for the events behind these diffuse gestures. Throughout his narration, he would

85

half-moan, stop short, and start again with "anyway"; and he uttered several half-sentences that ended not with words but with his biting the knuckle of his index finger. With a hand he would open, then ball back up in resignation and press against the ridge of his brow, he conveyed that his wife had cheated on him the night before and that he ought to have seen it coming. Though a self-styled rationalist, holder of an advanced degree in a field that could loosely be called science, he repeatedly invoked supernatural retribution, saying, "I deserved it," "I had it coming," and "What goes around comes around."

"Yeah," I repeated, in a near whisper, thinking my tone would soothe him.

He had been attending marriage counseling, he said. "But that's only added fuel to the fire. You know how those things go, people hear whatever they want. I swear to God, the therapist could say, you know, 'You need to be more attentive to each other's needs,' and she would turn around the next day and tell me, 'He told me I need to be more attentive to *my* needs.' The other day, she said to me, 'I'm a hostage to our relationship.' What the hell does that even mean?"

Looking back over her life, she saw that she had never had a hand in her destiny. Her father had been abusive, and had dragged her away from her friends and her grandmother, whom she loved, to Africa, where his religious fanaticism had turned their home into a prison. "This is the first I've heard of half of this," he said. "She always told me she'd loved being in Africa. She never said anything about any abuse." The years she had spent there, she told him, had made her feel a stranger in America, and when she returned, she was so lonely, she married a man she didn't love, simply because he paid attention to her.

This first husband was a failed businessman who spent their savings on a pyramid scheme and vanished, leaving her nothing but a home in foreclosure and boxes of pamphlets and video-cassettes meant to reveal the secrets of financial independence.

"I'm a mess," she told my father. "I need to work on myself."

Their counselor concurred: "Until her needs are met, your relationship will never be healthy. All couples must learn to grow together."

"I suppose it could be true," my father said to me.

His wife had begun to dress differently, wearing batik linen robes and turquoise pendants and bracelets of braided string. She slept in every day and neglected the housework. She joined a women's book club with an emphasis on "spirituality." Her counselor saw this as a "great step." Her prescription for Effexor had helped with her depression, but it also made her irritable and irrational. For this, she'd been given a mood stabilizer, then some other drug for the tremors it brought on. "This is the fucking irony of it," my father said. "Every day she's getting further and further into spiritual this and natural healing that, and in the meantime she's drugged to the goddamn gills."

My father's brow smoothed and its color returned as he eased into scientific jargon. He expatiated on the half-lives of drugs and their metabolic channels, on side effects, contraindications, and induced temporary psychoses. He seemed buoyant for a moment before slowing down and shivering. "So we went to this dinner party at our neighbor's, right," he began.

"We stuck around until everybody else had gone. Hell, I guess we polished off a couple of bottles of wine on our own. I know I was good and soused. She's not supposed to drink at all with the stuff she's on, but what can I do, she's a grown woman,

I'm not her boss. It was starting to get pretty late and I needed to go in early this morning, so I said, 'Look, guys, I'm going to pack it in.' Karen says to me, 'Well, do you mind if I stick around for a bit, I think Kent and I are going to smoke a joint.' I thought that was pretty weird, I mean, I can't believe I didn't just say, 'Hell no you're not sticking around to smoke a joint!' Whatever your attitude, it's still against the law, besides, I barely even know this guy, but like . . . it seemed pretty harmless at the time. Things have been so weird lately anyway with the therapy and all that, and we've been fighting so damn much, maybe I was just too exhausted to get into another argument at that hour. And for what? I just wanted to go home and get in bed."

He lowered his eyes in trepidation. He must have rehearsed this stage of the telling in his mind on the way over, and weighed the disgrace of it against the relief he hoped would accompany his confession. After a series of strange expressions—failed beginnings—had animated his face, his brows dropped, and, with a gasp, he pressed down the folds in his coat.

"It was four-fifteen in the morning. I turned over on my side and I saw those red numbers flashing on the alarm clock and now they're burned into my mind. I broke out in a cold sweat— like literally. I threw on a pair of jeans and a turtleneck and I ran to Kent's as fast as I could. I beat on the door until I thought I was going to knock it down. About two minutes later, Kent opened up, he was white as a damn sheet, and he starts saying, 'I'm sorry, I'm so sorry' over and over. Well, I just pushed past him and walked right in and said, 'Where the hell is my wife?' He backs away all scared and points up to the bedroom. I went up there, and man, the place was just trashed. There were empty liquor bottles and dirty ashtrays, the sheets were on the floor, and there were these . . . dildos and things everywhere. I was shouting Karen's name, I looked under the bed, back out in the hallway, and finally I yanked open the closet door in the guest bedroom and there she was, huddled down, trying to pull her panties up over her ankles. And you know what she said to me? You're not going to believe this. 'I thought the bathroom was in here.'"

"I thought the fucking bathroom was in here," he repeated, as if it was this phrase, and not her presumed philandering, that held the marrow of her betrayal.

9

My father spent the night. He was afraid to inconvenience me, offered to go sit at a Waffle House until my normal bedtime, and argued that he, and not I, should sleep in the living room. I insisted; I often slept there anyway, because it was closer to the fridge and I got thirsty at night. At last he said thanks and walked upstairs, sullen but probably happy for the uninterrupted rest. The night turned cold, and I wrapped my coat around myself before lying down on the futon. I thought a while about my stepmother, though it seemed strange to call her that, and about her amorous relations with the neighbor. My wool socks itched, and I kept stripping them off and then putting them back on when my toes started to go numb. When at last I was comfortable enough to drift off, my father began, in a manner, to boil. The shifting sheets hissed from the bedroom, and were shrugged off and irately bunched; a steady, nasal hornet's buzz cut through the crackle of snorts; and intermittently, he would bark mysterious strings of syllables: "Ashashashashashashashum." He was having a nightmare. It saddened me, and I wanted to wake him.

"Dad," I called out.

"Yes," he said lucidly, as though I had interrupted him in the midst of his duties.

I didn't try to speak to him again that night, and he shook and grunted till morning. I awoke to a note saying he'd had to leave for work, but that there was coffee in the pot for me. By then it had charred into crust, which I rinsed out in the sink. It was chilly, and yellow sunlight shone through the slits in the blinds. I looked at my books, stacked under a plastic bottle by the door, and thought I should spend the day making up my missed work. Then I lay down and went back to sleep.

10

In love, in desperation, we often put forth conditions; if they aren't met, things can't go on; but when someone sets doggedly to fulfilling them, this diligence only deepens our contempt. It was like this between my father and his wife. He spent a week at my apartment, then slunk back to her. In his absence, the marriage had only become more repulsive and insufferable; she insisted on having her own room, and said it was time they "open up" their relationship. In the afternoon, if I wasn't working, my father would drive by my apartment and call me from his mobile phone. He would invite me to the Taza de Oro, a newly opened coffee shop decorated with antique brewing instruments and burlap sacks stapled to the ceiling, each bearing the stamp of a plantation in pastel orange and sea green. He had found it on one of the walks he'd started taking after work to keep from returning home too early, and had taken a liking to the owner, a single father and veteran who had returned to Vietnam to consult in the coffee industry during the economic reforms in the late eighties. He had worked in management, but when he went out to visit the fields, he had fallen in love with "the idea of coffee," and, disillusioned with the business world, had retired early to open his own café. My father had a favorite table there, in the back, past the restrooms, with a blue wingback on one side of it and a matching ottoman on the other. He always ordered for me, and when he sat down would complain of Karen's most recent ultimatums, expelling a scornful "tsss" and swatting some unseen nuisance from in front of his nose. At around six he would hold his hand up and pinch his watch between his thumb and forefinger. Dropping his head, lifting his eyes, he would say he had to go.

For solace, he visited an internet chat room for "victims of infidelity." He told me about a woman named Nancy he met there. A social worker, she was married to a truck driver in a dismal town a few hours away. The truck driver stayed on the road for four- to five-day stretches, and when he came home on the weekends, he would sit on the couch and drink, watch porn, and brag about the women who'd invited him back to their homes while he was away. My father appreciated the chance to talk freely with Nancy, and I imagine she was drawn to his relative urbanity. Karen, whose disdain for my father's affections in no way diminished her jealousy of them, logged into his account one day while my father was at work and read their messages. When he came home, she was gone. A letter lay on the keyboard, the words smeared and veering off the lines of the paper. Amid obscenities and affronts, she told him he could die for all she cared, she hoped to never see him again, and she would take him for every cent he was worth.

The next day, my father was reviewing documents from an internal audit when he heard the growl of an approaching car. It stopped at the mailbox and idled, then took off with a grinding of gears. Soon after came an explosion of shattered glass and splintered boards. From the bay window, he saw Karen's car, half-destroyed, in the remains of the shed where they stored their lawn mower and gardening tools. She reversed, advanced again, and plowed into the collapsed mound.

My father ran outside and dragged her from the car. She was drunk and slurring, and a deep cut in her temple was spurting blood. He wrapped her head in a T-shirt and laid her in his backseat. She cursed him as he drove her to the hospital. They sedated her and sutured her wound, and my father filled in the forms for a forty-eight-hour involuntary commitment. When he was done, he came to my apartment, sat down at the side table in the kitchen, and began to cry. Everything about him seemed suffused with grief: the purple burst of capillaries in his porous nose, the waxy peak of his skull poking out from a whorl of disheveled hair. He pressed his face between his hands and hugged it with his eight fingers, each wisped with fine white hairs between the knuckles, and his pale, convex fingernails crossed his forehead in an arc, like ivory inlays in a diadem. I patted his shoulders and walked behind him to rub his back, with an embarrassed feeling, as though there were something false in my solemnity; but this did nothing to console him.

Once he had composed himself, he drove back to the hospital, but the staff, on Karen's orders, prohibited him from seeing her. He sat for hours in the waiting room, reading gossip magazines and drinking coffee from a machine. A policeman was called to escort him out, and when he returned to my apartment, quite early the next morning, he told me he had slept in his car on the roadside, because he hadn't wanted to wake me up but couldn't bear to go back home alone.

A week later he asked me to accompany him to retrieve a projector and a box of slides from a trip he had taken to Egypt with his own father, an engineer who had worked on the early

94

planning of the Aswan High Dam. "I've always wanted to share these with you," he said.

While we were in the kitchen going through boxes, Karen showed up with a swarthy, cadaverous man she introduced as Dr. Fisher. "He's a friend from my old job. He's helping me deal with all this," she said. Her manner was cool, but not hostile, with a sort of humiliated diffidence. Remaining in the doorway while her friend walked wordlessly to the bedroom, she asked my father to leave her in peace while she gathered a few of her things. She had filed for divorce, she told him—the papers would be coming any day now—and she would move out until everything was settled.

She took a number of my father's possessions, which then acquired enhanced significance in their absence—a coat tree in the shape of a sunflower and a ceramic lamp celebrating the signing of the Constitution: antiques that had been in the family a long time, he said. He found Dr. Fisher's number on the caller ID box and phoned Karen, begging her to return them. Amid her protestations, Dr. Fisher picked up on a second line.

"Don't you think you've hurt her enough?" he said.

"You listen here, you son of a bitch," my father said, shaking his fist at the receiver. "If you want to get in the middle of this, I've got something for you."

Mulling over the conversation later, my father remarked, "I've got six years of kung fu under my belt. I'd like to see him try and get a piece of me." He had studied it in graduate school, under an old Chinese man with rotten teeth whose picture I had seen in a magazine clipping my father showed me one night over dinner. I looked idly at my father's slope-shouldered frame, his soft arms, one with a vaccination scar like the impress of a dime, his long neck with its prominent Adam's apple, and tried to imagine him kicking like a windmill or jumping over his opponent's head onto a slanting roof, as I had seen the actors on *Kung Fu Theater* do on Saturday afternoons when I was a child.

It was "too much," my father said, to go back to the old house, and he stayed with me while he and Karen readied it for sale, each going over only when the other was away. On weekends, he would pay me to mow the lawn, dig up stumps, paint the shutters, or drag the fragments of the destroyed shed out to the street. As the sun thawed the frost and reflected in bright blurs from the blacktop, I'd take off my coat and hat, then my pullover, which was soaked with sweat. If he came back to pick me up before I was finished—most often, he used the time to run errands—he would walk in silence across the yard, hands pocketed, feet turned out in an awkward duck's step, or else go in the kitchen, sit in a chair, and caress some odd article—a framed feather from a trip to Costa Rica, or a ceramic mug with a jocose slogan—to grasp after the rich memories that transpired from it. In the mute blue of a late afternoon, when I was raking up and bagging brown mounds of crepitating leaves, he shut the door behind him and stood on the porch. His eyes, bright in their hollows, looked purposelessly around; then he asked me, "How's it going?"

"Not bad," I said. "I'll be done in a little."

He folded his forearms across his chest, clicked his tongue against the roof of his mouth, and looked down at the tawny toe of his furrowed shoe, pointing it up toward the porch light. His glasses fell off into his quickly proffered palm. So timidly that I shuddered, thinking him on the verge of suicide, he began: "You know, since everything with Karen started really going downhill, I've had no idea what to do with myself. It's like nothing has any meaning any more. Like there's no point in anything. I get up and I go to work and I come home and I go to bed, if you're working, maybe I go somewhere to watch a little TV. I have my coffee in the morning, a drink sometimes in the afternoon, read the paper, read my stuff for work, and the whole time, I'm just thinking, is this it, is this all there is? What's the point of my life on this planet? And so just today, while I was out, I was saying to myself, what do I have to lose any more? And I thought, to hell with it, you know. I'm going to enter the Body You Choose competition."

11

He went to the car and brought back a magazine called *Total Body Development.* He had dog-eared a six-page insert detailing the history and purpose of the competition. It encouraged entrants to "take the first steps in a lifelong journey away from the self-defeating behaviors that have kept you from having the body you've always wanted—and the life you've always dreamed of living." Competitors spent twelve weeks dieting and working out with the aid of supplements from Paradigm Fitness, the nutrition branch of the Total Body Development Corporation. They were judged on their physical progress, the goals they had set, and a two-hundred-word essay describing their motives for entering the contest and "the lessons they had learned along the way." Throughout were dubious before-and-after photos of entrants from previous years: on the left, they were hirsute and dejected, their faces sallow on gaunt necks drooping between hunched shoulders; on the right, they were shaved and striated, their limbs hard swells the tawny sheen of saddle leather, and their incandescent teeth glowed in truculent smiles beneath new hairdos, which were gelled stiff and golden, like the fins of fried fish.

He sent his form off the next day, and a week later his starter kit arrived. It included a Paradigm Fitness mail order catalogue, a booklet entitled *Secrets of the Champs*, with capsule biographies of previous winners and details of their workouts and diets, and a video: *Who We Were, What We Became: The Body You Choose Story.* It followed the lives of the four finalists in the first Body You Choose competition: Mack Richards, an ex-convict and janitor, who had entered, he said in an Alabama drawl, to give his mother a reason to be proud of him, because he'd disappointed her all her life; Earl Emmett, a drunk whose friends called him the life of the party—"That's the hardest part of it," he said, "knowing I'll have to leave all them behind and go it alone"; Tiffany Mistings, whose husband had died in a boating accident and who had spent the five years since living off his life insurance, eating ice cream, and watching soap operas for eight hours a day; and James Kremin, HIV-positive but "determined," as he said, "to beat this thing."

There were pitfalls, triumphs, and acrimony: Mack surpassed his end goal of fifteen chin-ups with four weeks in the contest to go. On their twentieth wedding anniversary, Earl's wife was sent to the hospital with seafood poisoning, and in desperation, he had "turned to the bottle." The cameraman interviewed him the following morning. He was shirtless, his body gone from corpulent to blocky and wading tentatively toward muscularity; but his dark eyes, into which he kept twisting his small, wizened fists, expressed horror at his looming failure. His chin shook, and he said this might be *it* for him; perhaps his alcoholism was stronger than his will to change, as he'd glumly feared all along. The next day Nathaniel Sweezey, CEO of Total Body Development, flew in his private jet to an airstrip in Earl's hometown of Norman, Oklahoma. He put his hand on the man's shoulder and said, "You cannot give up." This overwhelmed my father, and a tear welled in one of his eyes. He wiped it and stuck his finger in his mouth.

Near the end, there was a controversy. The contestants had been asked to submit, along with their essay, photos, and statement of goals, a drug test, which James Kremin failed. When Nathaniel Sweezey called him, James, obviously distraught, kept burbling, "It's for legitimate reasons," and, "My doctor told me to do it." A phone conference was arranged, and on a split screen, with Sweezey on the left and the doctor on the right, the topic of HIV-related hypogonadism was discussed. "We don't know the etiology of it, but it is a real condition," the doctor said. "With all the hype you hear in the news about 'roid rage and Ben Johnson and all that, people forget that steroids are legitimate medicine. Maybe some people abuse them, but that's not the case here, and unless you would be willing to disqualify other competitors for taking antidepressants or asthma medications—both of which could give them a leg up—then I don't see how you can disqualify James." He described the chronic weight loss, mood swings, and fatigue that plagued HIV sufferers, and concluded, "In my personal opinion, it is not James but the others who have an unfair advantage—they have healthy bodies and full lives ahead of them. James is fighting with everything he's got." Putting down the receiver, Sweezey looked at his brother Alan, the co-owner of the company. "We've got to let him stay," said Alan. Sweezey picked up the phone, called James, and said, "Hey man, we're back on."

Choosing the winners wasn't easy. "I've developed relationships with all these people," Nathaniel Sweezey told the camera. "It's like I'm rooting for all of them, and I'm the one who has to let them down." Nevertheless, in close consultation with his brother, he settled on Tiffany Mistings for the grand prize. At the start of the contest she'd been plump and pale, with an acne-spattered face and shoulders, and hair on her stomach and legs. By the finish she was lean and tan, with obtruding abdominals that reminded me of those dinner rolls sold stuck together in a pan at the supermarket. Her friends stood in the background catcalling and shouting "hottie" as she posed for the final photographs in a tenuous string bikini. Sweezey rang to tell her she'd won. After she screamed, dropped the phone, said thank you four times, and called her friends and family, a journalist from *Total Body Development* arrived to interview her. When he asked what she planned to do with the prize money, looking abashed, she took out a blue folder that had been resting between the pages of a phone book. "I never thought in a million years I'd win, but I promised myself if I did, this is what I would do," she said, and withdrew a sketch in colored pencil of a stone pedestal in the form of a swelling wave, with a bronze swordfish leaping from its crest. "For Andy's grave," she said, her voice breaking. "It's something I've been thinking about ever since it happened. He just loved the sea so much, you know."

The four finalists were flown to the Total Body Development headquarters in Scottsdale, Arizona. They toured the facility in golf carts, gave their final interviews, and checked into their resort, where each was assigned an individual Andalusian-style "casita," before a limousine picked them up for dinner. "Eat up," Nathaniel Sweezey said. "It's been twelve weeks, you deserve it." After a round of fried appetizers, they tied on plastic bibs, broke open their lobsters with silver crackers, and dipped the white meat lustily in ramekins of drawn butter. Raising a bottle of Coors Light, Nathaniel Sweezey proposed a toast. He talked about the road they had been down, what their achievements meant for the company; when he dreamed up the contest, he had no idea if it would flop. But they had stuck with it, they had made him proud; hell, he said, they were all winners, and he pointed with two fingers at a man standing to one side in a polo shirt and ball cap, holding a briefcase. As the man unclasped it and took out a pile of papers, Sweezey turned to his protégés and said, "These are endorsement contracts. If you want it, you're in. I'm bringing you guys on as representatives for the company."

"What did you think?" my father asked as the credits for the video began. Reflexively, I thought to say *great*, but worried it would be too transparently insincere. I grasped for other adjectives, for something, if not honest, then not absurd, and after equivocal remarks about the contestants' achievements, hit at last on the phrase, "pretty inspirational."

"I thought so too," my father said, resting his head contemplatively in his hand.

12

Although my father had, just after mailing his entry form, gone to the Vitamin Warehouse and bought several weeks' worth of whey and egg protein, creatine monohydrate, HMB, glutamine, and shark cartilage, the pressures in his life proved stronger than the inspiration the video afforded. He found it shameful for an adult to rent, particularly in an apartment complex, and he looked forward to buying a new home as soon as possible; but when he sought preapproval from a mortgage broker, his credit check revealed that Karen had taken out a number of high-interest loans without his knowledge. Several were already delinquent, and any future loans were contingent on their payment in full. He was disappointed, but not bitter. He still loved her, and talked occasionally over dinner about how deep their friendship had been, about the beauty of her eyes, and about the tender and humorous moments that had passed between them. When I went to bed, he sometimes called her; I could hear him just outside the door. At first, he would whisper commonplaces about his job and their shared acquaintances, then something she said would provoke him, and he would slam down the phone, cursing with indignation. The next morning he would pack his gym bag, determined to exercise after work, but some unforeseen delay would thwart him. As though in penitence, he would stop at the Vitamin Warehouse on the way home and buy a muscle magazine or a fat-burning beverage in a can; but at night, watching his favorite show, *The Pretender*, on a portable television brought from his old house, he would eat a whole bag of kettle-cooked potato chips and follow it with a pint of ice cream. One morning I saw him in his underwear, searching for a sock or maybe his wallet: with his soft, narrow shoulders, a brown birthmark between the blades, and his frame widening gently from the kidneys to the coccyx before dropping off into his thin, rigid legs, he looked like a bruised mango on a narrow, forking stalk.

His efforts to disentangle himself from his wife's debts proved futile, and he didn't have the money to pay them; so, instead of buying a home, he took a rental with an option to own. When the papers were signed, he asked me to move in with him. He said he always regretted that I'd had to work through school; he'd told himself when I was younger that he would put aside money to support me for these years, but things had gotten away from him; perhaps he could make up for that now. He offered me an allowance, not a lavish one, he admitted, but, so far as he could tell, I wasn't a spendthrift. I could have my own room and take his car if I needed in the evenings. He often had reports to review when he came home from work, and anyway, he wasn't much for going out.

The house lay in a bushy recess between a residential cul-de-sac and a parcel of woodlands fronted by a billboard splashed with the words *Development Opportunity!*, and it evinced the same bucolic pretensions that had drawn him to the home he'd shared with Karen. It charmed him to see the raccoons that dug through his trash at night, lifting food to their mouths in their

minuscule, slate-gray mitts. On his morning drive, he sometimes saw a doe. When the sun fell, he would open the sliding
glass doors that led onto the deck, cut on the porch lights, and
observe, his eyes close to the screen, the white-green bellies of
the luna moths that clung there.

I didn't tell him I had been placed on academic probation,
preferring again, though less calamitously than last time, to
register for the maximum number of credits in the spring, which,
if I made As in all of them, would raise my average to just under
a 3.0. I soon dropped one class, but within the time limit, so it
didn't count against me, and though I would later have nightmares
that I had left some detail unattended to and would be forced
to return home, to a town I no longer visited and an existence
I tried constantly to forget, I didn't fail, and would graduate three
years later with respectable if not boastworthy grades. I missed
being downtown: it was dull where my father lived, with nothing
distinguishing the rows of ranchers on their rectangular plots
between evenly spaced stands of replanted pines but the different colors of their facades and the occasional novelty mailbox
in the shape of a barn or Dalmatian. But the allowance and no
longer paying rent allowed me to cut down my shifts at work,
and when I threatened to quit because of a scheduling conflict,
my manager gave me a fifty-cents-an-hour raise.

My father and I traded the car during the week—some days
he would drop me off and pick me up, other days I had the car
from seven in the morning till six in the evening. If I had the
night off, after leaving him at home, I would drive to the Taza de
Oro to study. Business by then trickled down to a few eccentric
regulars: a shabby older man, fingers stained from nicotine, who
sat in a chair by the door reading tattered paperback editions of

Marcuse or Murray Bookchin and harangued whoever would listen with his unpersuasive anarchist dogmas; two men in their twenties who played dominoes for hours on end, less for the love of the game than as a pretext to insult each other; a beautiful though badly dressed girl with bobbed hair and sunken eyes, whom I'd had fantasies of asking out until she told me, the one time we conversed, that she was a proud Seventh-day Adventist. Glenn, the owner, stood behind the counter watching the news, or recollecting his years as a helicopter pilot in Vietnam if he had a listener, while his lissome daughter sat in the back, one foot on the floor and the other curled beneath her buttocks, clicking an ink pen and waiting for the phone to ring. From the back terrace, where I'd go to smoke, I could see the white flares of headlights, small as fleas, tailed by red speckles where the highway crossed the mountain, and nearer, a procession of eighteen-wheelers entering and exiting the pale radiance of a service station.

In less than a month, my father managed to slough off his abjection; I no longer saw him splayed red-eyed before the TV, with a trail of cracker crumbs embedded in his sweater. He went to the gym for cardio every morning and for weights in the afternoon. I imagined he had found inspiration in some article or essay, but he attributed his sudden vigor to a recipe for a shake he had found on the Body You Choose website. Developed by an Olympic trainer from the former Soviet Bloc, it consisted of one cup of oatmeal, one scoop of protein powder, a banana, a tablespoon of peanut butter, and one raw egg. He drank two of them a day, ate Paradigm Fitness protein bars at work, and gave up on cooked food almost entirely. "When I first started this thing," he said, "I was constantly asking myself, 'Should

I eat this?' 'Is it OK to have such-and-such?' The shake has just simplified things so much for me. Now I don't even have to think about food, it's totally out of my mind, and I can concentrate on my routine and on getting in enough active recovery."

Soon the mango shape began to lessen, then it disappeared entirely. Beneath the receding fat of his shoulders and biceps, hard bulges now arose; I saw them shifting, sometimes carving out a furrow, as he went shirtless through the house before breakfast, switching on the coffee pot or fetching his newspaper from the driveway. He bought new jeans after losing two inches from his waist, and began cuffing the sleeves on his T-shirts to show off his arms.

One Friday I got in late and slept into Saturday afternoon. When I woke and walked past the dining room table, I saw it greasy with furniture polish and set for three. My father was in the kitchen standing at the stove, sucking red sauce off a wooden spoon. "You going to be around tonight?" he asked.

"I guess so. Why?"

"Well," he said, pronouncing it *whale*—he was lapsing again into that languid accent, riddled with phrases like *good deal* and *okey-dokey*, that he resorted to when our conversations touched on something awkward. "I'm having someone over for dinner, and I thought it would be nice if you could join us."

"Who?"

"Nancy. You know, the woman from the online thing." This was another of his mannerisms—pretending he couldn't quite remember what he was talking about, and lapsing into imprecisions. "We've been emailing each other and doing the instant messaging thing on AOL. I feel bad for her, you know. She finally got around to leaving her husband, but the guy is a real son of a bitch, he's hassling her all the time, and even apart from that, trust me, no matter how bad a relationship is, it always hurts when it falls apart. So like, I got the feeling she could really use a friend. To be honest, I could, too."

He made it clear to me his intention was to "be there" for her and nothing more; not that he would mind, necessarily, if something came of it. She was a "very attractive lady," after all; but neither of them, he said, was looking to "rush into anything" with all they'd been through. "I need to keep my guard up," my father explained. "Hell, I'm not even through the divorce yet, that could take another four months." Amid many repetitions of the phrases "I mean" and "you know," my father detailed, as I stood there nodding and murmuring, the respective virtues and inconveniences of cohabitation and independence, furnishing himself, it seemed, with sufficiently robust accounts of each to permit him to celebrate his happiness if Nancy fell for him, and to brush it off if their meeting came to nothing.

"What are you making?" I asked.

"*Whale*, I have a little Italian sausage, some meatballs, some fresh pasta, that kind of thing."

"I thought you were doing the low-carb thing."

"Not all the time. Complex carbs I do, you need those for your workouts, but I put the kibosh on them after about four. Anyway, this is for you guys. I got a couple of chicken breasts for myself, I'll have those with some spinach and olive oil."

When he had seasoned the meal to his satisfaction and could leave it to simmer, he said he needed a shower and left the room. I walked out to the deck and pissed from the railing onto the tangle of kudzu eight feet below. It was warm for February, the rain had just stopped, and the plunking of water on the pavement and the car hood blended with the whisper of blown leaves. The clouds were breaking into broad, woolly plains, and sunlight was beginning to filter through. When I returned to the house, I lay on the floor and looked up at the sky through the blue square of window in the ceiling.

Nancy called, lost, from a succession of pay phones. This amused my father, and each time he picked up the phone, he laughed in two successive squawks, then snorted. "Yeah, we're really in the middle of nowhere out here," he said. Eventually he directed her to the Food King supermarket and told her to wait for him in the parking lot. He pressed the End Call button on the phone and rolled his eyes, thinking, it seemed to me, that he and his son must share the same benign derision for women and their purported failure to understand directions. I felt I was meant to make a similar face in return, but I couldn't bring myself to; I have always lacked the talent for these expressions of mutual sympathy. My father took his tan jacket from a hook by the kitchen door, raised his brows, and said, "Be back soon."

Ten minutes later, Nancy's white coupe was following his red sedan into the driveway, and across their windshields flashed the silver print of trees. When they got out, Nancy walked up behind him, put her arm around him, and they leaned into each other. My father stopped to say something, and the two of them glanced toward the house three or four times. I assumed he was preparing her to meet me, but could not imagine what he would tell her. Nancy was short and anemic-looking, with a head of neatly trimmed red curls; her mouth was slim and sad, her eyebrows thinly penciled, and she wore a long gray houndstooth overcoat. Stepping forward again, he held out his arm, and when she took it, his gait stiffened.

My father presented us to each other and said, "Why don't you have a seat at the table?" He opened a bottle of cabernet sauvignon he had read praise of in the Food and Wine column of the paper, and described to us its distinguishing characteristics, which didn't mean much to me but included the words *mouthfeel* and *finish*. After pouring two glasses, he said, "It should probably breathe a bit." He returned to the kitchen, plated the food, and laid it in front of us before bringing out his own monastic dinner and joining us.

After her first bite, Nancy looked heavenward and pressed a hand into her right breast. "Oh, this is wonderful," she said. "It's a crime you're not having any."

"Nope," my father said. "No bread, no pasta, no rice, no potatoes for now. Fruits, whole grains, and lean meats, that's my mantra. At least for the next seven weeks."

"No dessert?" she asked nasally.

"Not a chance."

"Well now you're just embarrassing me," she said, circling her waist with her hands. "I should probably do something like that, too."

"Nonsense," my father said. "You shouldn't change a thing."

"You know, your father has written me about you," Nancy said. "All wonderful stuff. You must be a very interesting person." She asked about my favorite books, and said that they, too, sounded interesting. "I wish I were still young, so I'd have time to read." She asked about school and what career I might choose, about my job, about what had convinced me to major in French. I gave tart replies, and after each one, a smile broadened across her lips; she looked to my father, who turned away and fawned at the empty air, narrowing his green eyes and showing his translucent teeth.

They were struck by numerous affinities that seemed to portend future happiness: they both loved bluegrass music, and they were both devoted fans of *The Pretender*. She glanced at the clock, clapped her hands, and said, "Oh my God, it's coming on in ten minutes!" My father cleared the dishes and sat beside her on the couch, carrying a cup of black coffee for himself and a slice of ice cream pie for her. He invited me to join them, but I declined; I wanted to get to bed early, I told them, though I knew the noise would keep me up. The show opened with Jarod, the protagonist, at a Tex-Mex restaurant, struggling to pronounce the word "chimichanga." Over lunch, he heard news of a young woman's disappearance, and went to the scene to pose as a "criminal behaviorist." I wondered how they could prefer this show among others from which it was substantially indistinguishable: even the script, from the prison interview with a prolix psychopath to lines like, "Every minute we stand here arguing is a minute closer to her death," seemed assembled from leftover parts. Once, amid a series of blunt blows, Nancy shrieked, and my father's croaking laughter followed. A few minutes later, I drifted off, while police sirens droned against string music in the background.

13

It had long been an ambition of the Weirdo's to disconnect my mother's phone. His inborn irascibility, coupled with his contempt for whatever human inclinations he did not share and his sense that no whimsy or pastime was too trifling to be judged in moral terms, blinded him to the attractions of any form of correspondence. His wish that others not be apprised of his doings he had elaborated into a general imperative to incuriosity, and back when I was still living with him and my mother, whenever I began a phone conversation with some school friend by asking the question, "Hey, what are you doing?" I could expect, without fail, that when I hung up, the Weirdo would ask me, "Hey, what do you care what someone else is doing?" Occasionally he would add, if I had gone on too long, "You see those fuckers every fucking day," or else he would tromp broodily to the garage to tinker with his tools, affecting an air of productivity detached from any concrete purpose. My mother had few friends and might not have minded the telephone's absence—surveys and telemarketers threw her into fits of rage—but she knew I was lonely, so far back on the mountain, and pleaded with the Weirdo that I needed the phone for group homework assignments, and later, to schedule dates. Sloth must have kept them from cutting the line in the year and a half since I'd moved away; but when I called my mother on the eve of her birthday, instead of a ringing, I heard a click, three shrill tones, and the soapy voice of the Time Lady reciting an intercept message lamenting that the number I had dialed was *disconnected or no longer in service.*

My mother worked as a receptionist at a dental clinic not far from my school. The next day, I skipped class and brought her flowers around noon. When I opened the door, a bell tied by a string to the door gave off a tinny chime, but my mother didn't look up, absorbed in a paperback with an image of Stonehenge on the cover of which she'd read two-thirds. She wore a strange hairstyle, tight at the temples and cloud-like on top with side combs an inch or two behind her ears. I watched her for a moment—her narrowed eyes, a licked index finger pressing the next page to be turned—then laid the bouquet in its crinkly cellophane on the desk. Her posture stiffened, and she looked at me with her lips parted, as though wishing to tell me something that demanded forethought. But then she smiled and said simply:

"Hey, you. What brings you here?"

I pointed to the flowers on her desk with the small *Happy Birthday* card pinned to them.

"How sweet of you."

"Thought maybe I could buy you lunch," I said.

She clenched her teeth and hissed through the interstices. "Oh, honey, I wish you had called. I'm taking a half-day today. I got Dan to agree to take me out, if you can believe that."

"I thought the Weirdo didn't do holidays."

"God, I wish you'd quit calling him that. It's been almost ten years now, if it wasn't funny before it certainly isn't now. Anyway, he's not as dogmatic as you act like, he just takes a little massaging."

Capable of ordinary human sentiment when massaged, I thought. What more could a woman ask for? And then I let myself say something mostly like that.

"A woman could ask for you not to be so nasty, for starters," my mother said. "He actually loves you and you never did give him a chance."

"You know your phone's disconnected, right? I did try to call."

"Well, I mean, you could have called here. I'm down here five days a week."

"It threw me off when I couldn't get through to you, I guess I didn't think about it. That's fine, though. Another day. I'll leave you to it . . . "

"My God but you're glum," my mother said. "Why don't you just come up afterward? We're not going to be down here till midnight. We could do burgers or something."

"I'll have to check with Dad. It's his car I'll be driving. Can I make a call from here?"

"Sure. Long as it's okay with Dr. Benjamin."

She went through the interior door, closing it behind her. Through the gap I saw a tall man with putty-like skin, a large head with a thin mantle of hair, and a white lab coat with a name embroidered in cursive on the pocket. "All yours," my mother said when she returned.

I called my father's cellphone. He was perplexed, showing exaggerated respect for my desire to spend time with my mother but uncertain as to how he would get home without me. When I told him my mother and the Weirdo would be spending the first part of the afternoon in town, he said he would call out for the rest of the day and I could come by whenever I liked.

"That sounded complicated," my mother said, hooking her arm through mine and guiding me toward the door. "Come outside with me, I've got to smoke."

She had twice changed brands since I was a child, from Vantages with their target logo, reminiscent of De Stijl, and the enigmatic hole in their filters; to Now 100s in the steel-gray soft pack with the futuristic font; to the long, thin More 120s with the dark brown wrapper. Once outside, she had to strike her lighter repeatedly until I cupped my hands around hers to screen her from the wind. Then she took a long and luxuriant drag.

"So what's up with you these days?" she asked, and I gave her the same answer as always.

"Why are you driving your dad around?"

"I'm staying with him, actually."

"Well, that must be a damn hoot."

"It's all right. He offered to let me till I finished school. So I wouldn't have to work so much."

"Is he still with what's-her-name?"

I put my hands in my pockets and took the time to survey the pale pavement with its black blotches of trampled gum. "Nah. She got sick or something."

"Well, he never was particularly fortunate in love. What's he doing now?"

"He's in this bodybuilding competition thing."

She laughed long, her face reddened, and she wiped away the beginnings of tears that smudged around her eyelids. "Oh dear God," she said. "I don't know why I act like I'm surprised, it's always something with him."

The Weirdo pulled up in his truck, a red 1960s Ford he'd painted by hand with a brush. He didn't get out. He turned to me in his cap, stamped with the logo of a tackle shop, and pinched and lowered the bill a half-inch to say hello. Then he looked ahead, resting his eyes on an office building or a traffic signal or the cars changing lanes up the road.

"My chauffeur's here," my mother said. "Look how he's dressed!" She pressed the stiff button on the handle, nearly level with her chin, and pulled open the door. The Weirdo, who preferred camouflage or earth-toned T-shirts and chinos, was wearing a polo and corduroys. The long sticker that indicated the pants' size still clung to his leg. My mother reached in, leaning on her front foot, and tore it off before asking me, "Isn't he dashing?"

"You coming too?" the Weirdo said to me.

"I don't think so!" my mother answered him, putting her hand to her chest, feigning offense. "This is our romantic afternoon out. Anyway, I can't have my son see me drinking, it's unsuitable."

"I'll be up later though," I told the Weirdo.

"Come around seven," my mother said. "That way I can get a nap in."

Citronella candles in tin buckets were lit along the porch to keep away the mosquitoes. My mother and the Weirdo were inside, but here, on a picnic table with a plastic cloth, was a jar of pickles, condiments in squeezable bottles, a "family-size" bag of rippled potato chips, and a yellow plastic tub of French onion dip. When I went inside, I found the Weirdo pressing divots into beef patties with his thumb while my mother watched *Forensic Files*. Ellie, their Labrador, hurried over, her nails clacking on the hardwood floor. I bent down and kissed her where her skull dipped between her eyes and rubbed the soft nap of her ears between my fingers and palms.

"Hey, boy," the Weirdo said. "You ready to eat some little bunnies?" He had enjoyed tormenting me with this question since he'd first built the rabbit hutches when I was twelve or thirteen.

"I think I'll pass," I said.

"Yeah, I reckoned you might say that."

"You still keeping them, though?"

"Yeaaah. They're getting to be more trouble than they're worth though. Just feedin' 'em isn't cheap. Then I had a ol' raccoon kept gettin' in there, hell, you can't keep a raccoon out of a damn cage. They'll eat the babies, you know. I finally trapped him, but then, shit, what are you gonna do with him? I tried to feed him poison, he wouldn't take it. Stuck a knife in there, he bled all over the place, started shrieking, but I'll bet you could stab a raccoon twenty times and not kill it. Finally I just dropped the cage in the pond out there and let it sit in there till it drowned. Don't really give you a warm fuzzy feeling."

"I guess not," I said. "What else have you been up to?"

"Ah, you know. The wonderful world of laying tile. Not much about it you'd be too interested in hearing, I figure."

"His father's becoming a bodybuilder," my mother shouted from the sofa.

"It's not a real bodybuilding competition," I said. "It's one of those change-your-body-in-twelve-weeks things like you see in the magazines, with the before-and-after photos and all. He got the idea after him and Karen split up."

"Is Karen the bitch?" my mother asked.

"No, Karen's his most recent wife, I don't know if you met her."

"Yeah. I can't hardly keep up."

My mother went on poking fun at my father after she'd turned off the TV and we'd gone outside and sat at the table. While the Weirdo was arranging the beef across a griddle placed over bricks, she told the story of my father's ill-fated foray into gardening: "I'll never forget, this was I guess a year or two before you were born, and we had just moved out of our apartment because your father *had to* have a house with a yard. I guess he saw himself as the proud yeoman sitting on his porch smoking a pipe and watching his lands bear fruit. Well sure enough, I look out the window one day and there he is with a goddamn rented tiller tearing up a perfectly good patch of lawn. Just let it go, I said to myself, there's no point in my going out there and pissing all over his parade. I'd tried to tell him before, a garden is work, you don't just throw a couple of seeds in the ground and wait around for nature's bountiful harvest. An hour later he runs into the house and takes me by the hand and drags me outside, 'You've got to see this,' he tells me, and when we cross the driveway he falls down on his knees like he's praying, and he tells me with that snotty tone he gets, 'And you told me nothing would grow here.' Then he digs his hands into the dirt, raises them up to the sky and lets it crumble through his fingers, and he says, 'Look at this fine, rich soil.' Now I'll be goddamned if it wasn't coal dust from when the old owners used to dump out their ashes back before the house had electric heating. I tried to tell him as much, he just got all pissed off and said I didn't have a clue what I was talking about."

"So then what?"

"Oh, he planted a regular Garden of Eden out there. He kept his hopes up a good four or five months. He'd go out every day and stand there and stare, pull up some grass and weeds and get level with the ground to see if there were any shoots growing. Now and then he'd hit it with the hose. It was ages before he gave up."

"When did you know it wasn't going to work with you and Dad?" I asked.

"I guess when I couldn't stop vomiting on my wedding day!" my mother replied. "It just wasn't in the cards for me and your father. I think the thing I liked most about him was he had a car. When we met, I'd just gone back to stay with my mother, you can imagine what fun that was, me with scarcely a penny to my name and her drunk half the time. And your father can be very seductive, he comes across as this sort of charming intellectual type. Or maybe he really is that, who am I to say. The point is, it just didn't work out."

While she spoke, the Weirdo lifted the collar of his T-shirt and retrieved a Marlboro from the box stuck to his chest (he had begun carrying his cigarettes in this novel manner one day when he was shirtless doing yardwork and discovered a thin sheen of sweat was enough to make the cellophane cling to his skin). When he was done smoking, he stubbed his filter out in a gob of mayonnaise and dragged it in circles and spirals around his plate.

"I'll wash up," I said, standing and gathering the plates, but my mother told me not to bother, that they'd load them into the dishwasher after I left.

"You got a minute?" the Weirdo asked me. "I'd like to show you something."

He led me down the porch stairs and around the garage, to the trail leading into the woods. We walked for twenty or thirty yards into a sort of clearing. He had cut down most of the trees there. The yet-to-be-uprooted stumps stood haggard at the height of my knees, and the branches of the still-standing hickories and chestnuts were strung with ropes and thin chains threaded through the gray plastic disks of a home weight set.

"Beautiful, right?" he asked.

"What is it?"

"Ah hell," he said and burst out laughing, covering his mouth with one hand. "It's this thing I seen on TV, one of these projects you sort of get in your head. They had this show about ornamental trees, these guys had hung weights from the branches and they bent 'em into all sorts of shapes. Looked really nice, so I picked up this old weight set from the salvage shop thinkin' I'd try and do some kind of arbor out here. But I've had 'em hanging there for months and the trees don't look a damn bit different, I guess I'd have to say I need something heavier. I's thinking if your Dad's into bodybuilding, maybe he could have the weights then, I'd be happy to run 'em down for him."

"I don't know," I said. "He seems pretty wedded to his gym routine. He may not have the room, either. I'll ask him though."

"Sure. It was just something that occurred to me," the Weirdo said.

There was a stone next to the driveway where he liked to sit and stare down into the gulley. He took his place there while I walked back into the house to say goodbye to my mother. I found her lying on the couch, already asleep, with the television still on and the dog curled up on the floor below her. I took a Coke from the refrigerator for the road and went outside and got in my car. The Weirdo saluted me with two fingers to his temple, then came over and rested a forearm on the window frame. I tried to shake his hand, but he leaned in, pulled me toward him, hugged his shoulders to mine, and patted me on the cheek.

"You be good now," he said to me.

"You do the same," I replied, then took off on the long drive back home.

14

It was possible to divine in my father the grains of some future action in the attitudes he adopted toward his defects. If he touched the top of his head ruefully, stroking the crest of it with his two middle fingers, or bent down to glance at his bald spot in the rearview mirror before driving away, the postman would soon show up with pamphlets on hair transplant clinics and micro-pigmentation—in the end, for reasons of economy, my father settled on a wax-based scalp concealer: a brown crayon, in essence, which he used only once before throwing it away. When he pinched his belly while sitting at breakfast, it was inevitable that, not long afterward, he would describe to me his meeting with a plastic surgeon, and the risks and benefits of the three types of liposuction: tumescent, laser-assisted, and super-wet. His general sensation of bodily displeasure, an apparent consequence of the contest, seemed to grow as, after a period of rapid transformation, his progress plateaued. "It's normal, they say," he mused one day over his midafternoon omelet, "but at the same time, I've got to power through, it's not like I've got all year." He was already near the halfway point. To the general accumulation of apparatus—the scale, the shaker bottle with the wire globe inside for crushing clumps of protein powder—was added what looked like the claw of a robotic lobster, a digital skinfold caliper, used to measure the percentage of body fat. For several days running, my father drearily clasped his love handles, his abdomen, the skin above his nipples and knees, and ran the results through an equation. Displeased with the results, he switched first to the seven-site, then to the nine-site technique. I had to take the measurements from his triceps, lower back, and scapula, which he couldn't reach. "Easy now," he would say, or "Be careful, damn it," afraid I was skewing the results by pulling up too much skin or stretching it too far from his body. A week later, with not a pound of muscle gained or fat lost, he said, "I can't do all this myself," and turned to the Yellow Pages to look for a trainer.

The listings were few, and many looked dubious: Twenty-Second Century Fitness advertised fifteen-minute sessions of Electro-Muscular Stimulation for forty-five dollars an hour; the Muscle Plant, a vegetarian bodybuilding outfit, had a half-page ad that showed a gorilla chewing a stalk of bamboo and a gangly kid in shorts—the setting for this implausible encounter was not made clear—with the sarcastic question, "How do you expect to gain muscle if you don't eat any protein?" My father made a short list and began calling; some numbers were disconnected, some trainers' schedules full. The two appointments he made, both for the next morning, could not have been more disappointing. The first coach was a "coot" in his sixties with polyester pants pulled up to his nipples and a basement gym stocked with antediluvian equipment, including a "three-spring chest expander" of which my father remarked, "No thanks. I already pulled out the few chest hairs I had with one of those things when I was in high school." The second barked at my father like a drill sergeant, called out exercises with no rhyme or reason, and counted his repetitions in a booming voice, which my father hated. "I did linear regression analysis in my doc program," he said. "I don't need some mouth-breathing idiot to count for me." Worse, the man had mocked his regimen of Total Body Development supplements, encouraging him to throw them all out and take up a diet centered on raw almonds and several pounds a day of canned salmon.

After airing his irritation, my father stomped off to the bedroom, and I shouted that I was taking his car out for an hour. I had been antsy since waking, there was nothing in the refrigerator but haddock filets, mustard, and milk, and I had barely eaten the night before. I drove to Giffone's, a Greek restaurant with an Italian name, overseen by a hairy, despotic husband, his meek, solicitous wife, and their three teenage children, all identical but for slight variations in stature. I sat, as always when it was available, at the booth facing the corkboard with its wavy paper frame where an affluence of surely doomed businesses posted their adverts and cards. Realtors abounded, as did plumbers and locksmiths, some of whom hawked their talents with clever mottoes, others with proclamations of their unrivaled reliability, of twenty-four-, or even, for one enterprising tradesman, twenty-five-hour-a-day availability. The larger flyers, photocopies in black-and-white or printouts in the pale ink of cheap home printers, tended to discretion, but today a slick red one was taped over the rest, almost glowing in the dead center, as though in triumph over its vanquished rivals. In a disorienting but compositionally agreeable montage, it showed a bodybuilder in a black leather vest and pants sitting on a throne holding a flintlock musket, and next to him, a muscular bikini model in a thong with her back turned, black hair fanned out over the wings tattooed on her shoulders. In letters that mimicked diamond plate steel, tinted in sex-appropriate pink and gray, were the words *3x NPC Top Five Finisher, 2x Women's NPC Physique Winner, IFBB Elite Pro Women's Fitness Competitor*, and, further down, *Gunn & Grace*, with a phone number and email address.

"Can I ask you a question?" I said to the smallest of the vassals when he came by to clear my dish.

He nodded, shifting his overlong bangs momentarily from his eyes, blinked, and said, "Yes."

"Any way I could take that flyer with me?"

"Oh Lord yes, hon," his mother answered, appearing promptly next to him and laying a rumpled hand on the shoulder of his stiff white shirt. "I've hated it ever since they put it up there, but you know, they covered it in packing tape and I've just been too lazy to bother with it. Georgie, go ask your father for a box cutter and take that ad down for this young man."

The boy walked away, arms stationary at his sides.

When I presented my father with it later, he said, "Hm. Pretty impressive, actually. The girl even more than the guy. IFBB, that's the top of the top."

"They look kind of terrifying," I said.

"It's probably just a marketing thing. For me this is about health and learning to improve my outlook, but you've got to realize, it's still bodybuilding. A lot of these guys are like cavemen, their whole outlook is be the alpha male, pick up the biggest rock, kill all the weaklings, get the hottest girl. And even if these two aren't like that, they've got to appeal to people who are. What the hell? It can't hurt to call."

My father walked to the kitchen and picked up the cordless phone. Soon after he dialed, I heard cacophony, grindcore or thrashcore or some other subgenre of -core music dimly relayed through the receiver. Two times my father repeated his request for an appointment the following day, but Gunn or Grace could neither hear him nor apprehend that lowering their stereo's volume temporarily might ease communication. My father groaned "For God's sake" and walked out to the driveway, where he could scream into the handset without my staring at him. Returning thirty seconds later, he announced: "Good news. I'm on for noon tomorrow."

I was meant to pick up my check that day, and my father agreed that I could take the car after dropping him off. Gunn and Grace was located on the side of a four-lane thoroughfare in a stand-alone brick building, a former barbershop or luncheonette. The windows were covered with mirror sheet, and a motorcycle with ape hangers and a flaming skull on the gas tank stood parked by the door.

"Come in and say hi," my father said when I didn't cut the engine.

I got out and pushed open their door, triggering a motion-sensor chime that produced the roar of a lion.

Gunn—could that really have been his name?—was leaning on a glass display case filled with fingerless gloves, ball caps, and pill bottles adorned with pictures of molecules, looking at a copy of *Soldier of Fortune*. My father told him he had called for a session; he stuck out his hand and said, "Cody Gunn. Nice to meet you. And congrats."

"For what?" my father asked.

"You made it in, bro. That's the hardest step."

He looked like the comic-book character the Swamp Thing. A plethora of tattoos covered the exposed flesh below his neck, so tightly drawn as to be hardly distinguishable, giving his skin a green tint like that of algae: looking closer, I saw among them a snub-nose revolver and a set of brass knuckles with the letters K-I-L-L in the rings. He wore a black tank top with the Morbid Angel logo, black athletic shorts, and black high-top sneakers.

"You brought a little buddy along?" he asked.

"This is my son," my father said.

"Ah, yeah? You lookin' to get jacked too?" Cody asked.

"No."

"I don't know, bro. You got a good frame. A couple of months throwin' that iron around, you could have the chicks lining up around the block."

I ignored him. "I'm going to run to work," I told my father. "I'll stop back in for you in an hour," I said.

"Make it an hour and a half," Cody interrupted. "My second afternoon client bailed, so I'm gonna put your old man to the test."

I wonder whether it was displaced sadism, the cycle of abuse they talk about on the news, or the thought of diluting his impending plight that compelled my father to ask me to stay, and to suggest, when I objected I had nothing to wear, that I take his credit card to the Kmart across the street to buy a pair of sweat shorts. "Christ," I whispered between clenched teeth as I leaned forward to retrieve it. Cody made a fist and said, "Hell yeah. That's what I'm talking about."

I stayed gone as long as was plausible, glancing through the CDs and attempting to use the bathroom, which was occupied by a panting, groaning figure whose masturbatory endurance or obstinate constipation outlasted my willingness to wait. I changed in the dressing room and wore the shorts out of the store. When I returned to the "training laboratory," as it was called, I found Gunn standing, arms akimbo, over my father in the plank position with sweat pooling on the floor beneath his face. "Keep holding it like that," Gunn said, "and don't you dare drop down on your knees. I'm gonna take care of the little man right quick."

Gunn whistled, and the woman I had seen with him on the poster emerged from a doorway in the back of the room. "Grace," he said, "I want you to run this kid through the wringer, show him what's up. I'm working on his old man over here."

"No problem," she said, and smiled with practiced seductiveness.

"Hey kid," Gunn said. "She's taken, so don't let me look over there and see a little banana popping up out of those new shorts of yours."

Grace walked to a corner by a set of wall bars and told me to warm up with twenty push-ups. As I obeyed, she shouted a series of postural modifications—"back straight," "elbows in," "feet together," "head up"—that seemed designed to make the movement impossible. When I fell flat, she dropped to the floor and started doing them as well, rising off the floor and clapping between each repetition.

"You really want to let a girl smoke your ass like this?" she asked.

"I don't care," I said.

"OK, now give me twenty sit-ups."

Now and again I looked over at my father, who was maneuvering an assortment of different-sized cast iron balls with teardrop-shaped handles on top. Now he posed on one leg, with the other extended behind him, trying to lift one off the floor;

128

now he was squatting, nearly falling each time, then leaping holding another, heavier one over his head. It seemed more entertaining than the tasks I was assigned: hanging from a bar while the dominatrix counted off the seconds or running back and forth through an arrangement of tires; but when I caught sight of my father's flushed face, he wore an expression of consummate despair, and soon he ran off to a trash can to vomit. Our ordeal ended with a series of calisthenics performed side by side, while Gunn and Grace stood before us smirking and snapping their fingers when we were due to change movements.

I walked outside as soon as we were done. My father hung back to pay. "I'll tell you what," he said when he emerged, "that guy's the real fucking deal." I unlocked the door for him, and he flopped inside, immediately reclining the seat. "How was it for you?"

"Horrible," I said.

He fell asleep when we reached the highway, and I had to shake him awake when we got home. He went into the kitchen, opened a Diet Coke, took a sip, and left it on the counter. He sat in his easy chair, pulling a lever to raise the spring-loaded ottoman beneath his feet.

"So you're gonna go back?" I asked him.

"Yeah," he chuckled. "I made an appointment for tomorrow." He was daunted, but also seemed pleased with himself. He said he was too tired to make dinner that evening, but offered to pay for takeout if I didn't mind driving to pick it up. He pulled out two twenty-dollar bills and asked for three hamburgers without the bun. The restaurant was close by, but I drove past it and onto the newly opened ridge cut, listening to music and observing the last light of evening. When I reached the bridge to downtown, I pulled off and turned around, taking the slow route back to the tavern. While I waited on our order, I played a game of pinball. I made it back home around eight. I announced myself at the door, but my father didn't answer. He was lying inert in the living room, right where I'd left him, a white foam of saliva in the corner of his lips. On the TV, two men in suits were screaming at one another about the ethics of bombing a country I'd never heard of. I left his food in the bag, put it in the oven, and took my meal to my room.

When I awoke the next day, my father was snoring in his room. I carried my books out onto the deck, where I could read through his snorts and wheezes, which were too irregular to ignore. I heard him groan and stomp into the living room a few hours later. I looked back through the sliding glass door and saw him bent and holding his knees like Allen Joseph in *Eraserhead* before pulling himself up and stumbling outside.

"God, I'm fucking crippled," he said.

I went in to make him a pot of coffee while he called out from work, claiming he was running a fever. As it brewed, I asked him how he would make it through training that day.

"To hell with that," he said. "I'm canceling my appointment."

I poured him a cup of coffee and took him the phone. After he dialed, I heard Gunn scream on the other line. I could only make out a few words: *bro, bitch, pussy,* and the affirmation *You've already made it through the hard part.* "Listen," my father told him, "I can't just go in there and kill myself then sleep twelve hours a day, I have other things going on in my life. Plus rest and recovery is just as important as working out . . . " He trailed off here, ceding to Gunn, who had not stopped raving. Eventually my father hung up and tossed the phone onto the couch.

"Whatever. I tried it," he said, then began adducing excuses: you grow muscle in your off time, not when you're in the gym; studies show that the majority of lifters are actually overtrained; and so forth.

"You don't have to convince me," I said. "I thought that guy was a moron."

"Yeah," my father laughed. "No pain, no brain, I guess."

He took a nap that afternoon when I went to class. When I returned, I found him at the dining room table studying his deluxe hardcover of Boyer Coe's *Getting Strong, Looking Strong: A Guide to Successful Bodybuilding* and making lists of exercises with his Pelikan fountain pen. He shrugged when he saw me come in.

"Back to the drawing board," he said.

15

Fox: I associate her name with certain casts of sky, in particular a blue-black one with whitish tufts of cloud poking out like puffs of piling from a threadbare sofa. Not from the day we met, of which I remember little but the sight of her in three-quarter profile, eye makeup in filigree extending almost to her ear, and then my initial, for me unusually bold, approach to her to ask for a cigarette, and her mocking laughter through gapped teeth as I lit it, on account of my liking the Rollins Band, whose name was printed on my shirt. The sky in question is from a night sometime later, two or three weeks before we slept together, when she still had a boyfriend, a bantamweight rockabilly type with a large, almost oblong head that was resistant, unlike my own, to the incursions of pattern hair loss. I met her out—she had invited me when I ran into her in the student center, and I hoped, since her remarks about her boyfriend were unflattering, that she would decide to spend the night with me. After a few beers, I got her to step outside to smoke and walk as far as the graveled levee that rose over two depressions thick with unmowed grass and typha and to the back parking lot of my building. But when I reached for her hand, she pulled away impishly, flashed a V with her index and middle finger, and jogged back the way we had come. At work the next day, at one of the college cafeterias, the woman who stood beside me on the belt, removing the cups and silver from the students' trays before I dumped their leftovers in the trash, asked me how my date had gone. I told her Fox had a boyfriend, that she'd met me at a bar but had run off when I'd tried to take her home. "You a damn fool," she said, "she waiting for you to kiss her. If not she wouldn't have wanted to meet you." This may have been true, but the air had felt so dense, and my will was so weak, and I didn't have enough warning before she turned back.

There was utility for her in our—I shouldn't say romance, to avoid ostentation, or hookup, which feels trite. There was utility for her in the implied obligations that sex is meant to carry in its wake. She had fallen out with her roommate and needed to move, her boyfriend told her she couldn't stay with him, and when she called me, less distressed than I would have thought, I said I didn't mind if she shared my studio, I was almost never there. I picked her up a day or two later and we watched something on the VCR, I don't know what but my taste at the time was for the pretentious or self-consciously trashy; we leaned closer in, shared a blanket when it got cold, and when she kissed me, bored with my wavering, I told her I had "trust issues." She giggled, and that made me less afraid.

In the morning, I drove her to her rental, a mobile home with an add-on porch and skirting over the wheels, to pick up her things while her roommate was at work. Nothing was in boxes, nor were there boxes waiting to be filled; her clothing lay piled in the bottom of a hall closet, and her books—among them *Tally's Corner*, *The Second Sex*, and *In the Freud Archives*—lay across the floor, as if thrown aside after reading. We gathered it all in our arms and dumped it in the trunk of my car. She apologized

133

for the disorder; I told her not to worry, cupped her ears in my hands, and ran my nose along the part in her hair. I would like to describe the rest, *making love to* or *fucking* her, but it no more yields to narrative than the truth of painting to ekphrasis; the words that come to mind to characterize her body range from pornographic to prissy, and in their vulgarity or their scruples they fail; to invoke love, which is right, is at the same time to duck these dilemmas, and it is perhaps for this reason, for this need of a diversion to provide the sidelong view that strangely makes everything clearer, that I cannot think of her without some atmospheric effect that endues her with the right measure of elusiveness.

We were not happy together; I didn't for that reason desire her any less. Money would have helped; at least then we could have gone out more or decorated the apartment; but money was not forthcoming, not from my work-study and not from her job at the cash register of a supermarket. My mother did send me a check on birthdays or holidays; I don't know if Fox's family could have managed to do the same. I visited them with her once: they brought to mind those gruesome stories you read in newspapers of people living off in the hills, intermarrying and hunting small game and signing their names with an X. On the outside of their house, wet rot had eaten away the corners of their doorframes and ledges, and the inside was covered in dust. Their few modern conveniences were disconsonant, giving no impression of any conceivable form of life, looking rather like fetishes from a cargo cult, and they spoke with awe of their daughter going to study in "the city"—a town of forty thousand during the school year, twenty thousand in the summer—as if she had escaped to the moon.

Fox didn't have a driver's license, and I took her back and forth to school and work, went to my own job, attended and then stopped attending classes. I would sit alone for hours in my white room, staring at the stains around the light switch, making lists, if my mood lifted, of languages I would someday learn and countries I would someday visit. I pepped up when Fox was home, at first for the novel charms of domesticity, after a month or two just for sex. When I cooked for us—which she couldn't do—or bought groceries—which she wouldn't, preferring to save her money for books or cosmetics—I hissed and sighed and she asked what my problem was, and I said nothing because I was afraid of loneliness. Things might have lasted that way a long time had my car not broken down and brought the dull drama to a close. One day, I heard a crackling, like a can being crushed, and the thing stopped accelerating; the transmission, a garage owner told me after a tow, would cost two thousand dollars to replace. At the time I had two hundred, Fox no more than fifty, and my mother was emphatic that she wouldn't help. I took the three hundred dollars the mechanic offered me for parts. For a while I tried to convince myself I had the initiative to regularly walk the hour and a half to school and work; Fox, under no such illusion, left immediately to stay with an acquaintance. Just after the beginning of the spring quarter, I called home in sorrow, and my mother said the Weirdo would come and get me and my things. I cried and told Fox I was sorry, that I felt that I'd failed her; I believed her reliance on me bespoke a vital ineptitude in her and not merely an idle character that preferred dependency when possible but otherwise was capable of initiative; she didn't seem much to care, and hugged and kissed me desultorily.

I proposed we stay together. We were only three hundred miles apart. Fox agreed, but neither of us discussed what this might mean. I didn't have my own computer, and had to check my email at the library. I was more affectionate in prose than over the phone, not that either of us could afford to pay to call long-distance too often. Her emails grew less frequent, some days no more than a line, and when her protests that she still cared for me, that she loved me, rang false, I logged into her account and found a message from someone named Jake asking her if she wanted to come over for "more hot tub action." I cut and pasted it and mailed it back to her, and she replied with a message with the subject line READING MY EMAIL!!!! We talked, argued about which of us had committed the worse betrayal, and insulted each other when the argument led nowhere. The natural thing would have been not to talk again, but either we weren't really so angry or we were unsuited to grudge-holding, and in a series of conversations followed by cheap presents in the mail, we agreed to continue as friends.

I called Fox one day from my father's house and asked if she felt like coming to visit.

"How am I going to get up there?"

"You could take the bus."

"Great idea. I can't think of anything more worth my time than hopping on a Greyhound with a bunch of psychos and drug dealers so I can get raped and murdered behind a service station in some jerkwater burg in the middle of Arkansas."

"I can't come get you. I don't have a car right now."

"You could come see *me*. You could even come this weekend?"

"It's short notice," I said. "I'm scheduled to work."

"Try and get off. I'll take you to see pro wrestling."

"Wow. My life's dream."

"I'm serious," she said. "This dude who comes to the store is always telling me he can get me in. I don't think it's like the stuff on TV, this guy looks like a rhinoceros and he's always got bruises and cuts all over him. It'll be something for us to laugh at, and we can kill two birds with one stone: you'll get laid for probably the first time since you last saw me, and my eight-foot-tall stalker will meet my pretend boyfriend and maybe stay off my back."

It stung me that she was so glib about sex, which I feigned then to consider precious because I hadn't had enough of it to make it mundane, and it hurt me too that for her I was the incidental pretext for an act I could scarcely imagine without her. But my indignation didn't prevent me from thinking of her naked, from reviewing her in my mind with wonderment and recalling how it felt to take her in my arms, and so I said, pretending indifference, my heart pounding unpleasantly, "Let me talk to work and see what I can do."

Getting off was easy. Two shifts I gave to Jerry, whose supposed electronics business had gone under, and who was trying to earn extra cash for his "monthiversary" with his new girlfriend (when Joe had said to him, "Be honest, Jerry, how do y'all even do it, with you bein' so fat?" Jerry had warbled back to him, "Well, ah mostly do stay on bottom"). Another my manager told me not to worry about—he needed to cut labor by 5 percent that quarter if he hoped to make bonus.

The awkward or inflated enthusiasm that characterized many of my father's responses to the aims or interests I expressed during the year or two we lived together was observable as I told him of my plan. I didn't mention Fox, I just said I was thinking of spending the weekend away to visit friends from my freshman year. "I don't suppose one of these friends might be a young lady?" he asked, and his brows and lower lip rose in unison, as if tugged on by a string. "I might see Fox, the girl I used to go out with," I replied, and he squinted and gave a sly nod that seemed to connote some sort of inter-male complicity.

"How are you doing as far as money?" he asked.

"I mean, OK," I said.

"How about if I take care of your ticket?"

"Sure. That would be great."

Two days later, my father drove me to the bus station. It lay at a distance, on the way to the airport, three miles north of the old CESID offices. My father hadn't spoken of the business since his relationship with Karen had come to an end, and it never seemed judicious to ask. But I sensed some willingness in him as we approached the location and he pointed at the sign to the music store with its repugnant, goggle-eyed glower and said, "I've always hated that damn thing."

"It really is hideous," I said.

"For all I care, this entire strip mall could sink into the ground."

"What did you end up doing with the business anyway?"

"Hell, I haven't done anything with it, strictly speaking. The business is Karen's—it's her name on it—though the bills are still coming out of my account, of course. As far as the assets—which don't exist, for all intents and purposes—that's something the lawyers will have to work out in the divorce. I'm hoping she doesn't make it too hard on me, but it's impossible to say, she's so moody. She told me she doesn't want to talk, and honestly that suits me fine, right now. I'll finish the contest, she'll do whatever she's got to do, and I guess we'll see if we can deal with everything like adults when this blows over."

"No chance you'll get back together, then?"

"Nooooo." He drew the word out, modulating the vowels like a battery-powered ghost in a haunted house. "I can't even imagine how we would go about trying to reconcile. Don't get me wrong, I'm not elated about adding another divorce to the record, not sure what that says about me, but at the same time, you've got to be honest with yourself sometimes and say, it's over."

My father pulled into the lot of an erstwhile chain store, now dingy and lurid, which housed a combination charity thrift store and evangelical megachurch. "Sorry," he said, "don't want to get this all over the side of the car," and he dumped his plastic mug of coffee out the window. Then he drove through thin woods with grass frontage that gave off a not-quite-natural glow. Every hundred feet or so was a one-family home with a carport or the squat brick premises of a post office or fraternal organization.

The airport was visible from the bus station. Because of consolidation or mergers or some other inscrutable financial machination, it had entered into apparently irremediable decline years before, and now, apart from one route to Chicago and another to Dallas, it served only charter services and a handful of Cessna hobbyists. The bus station, by contrast, had the feel of a bazaar. Men, looking gruff, humble, or humiliated, wandered back and forth through the flapping double doors to confer with the family members who had driven them there; there were fewer women, and most of them wore pink or powder blue garments suited to exercise or slumber. The majority would be bound for Atlanta, generally the first stopping point for people from my hometown who meant to run away; I would go on another hundred miles south and west, and had brought for the journey a self-improvement project: a copy of *Germinal* and a bilingual dictionary.

My father accompanied me inside after parking.

"Good thing we got your ticket over the phone," he said, pointing to a line of eight or ten people huffing and sighing behind a customer whose improbable tale of a lost ticket purchased on the credit card of a relative whose last name he didn't recall inspired equal parts incredulity and pity.

"Probably every one of those dudes is going to try that exact same bullshit," I said.

"You want something to eat, a bottle of water before you go?" my father asked. But I didn't care for the ominous name or appearance of the Terminal Grille, where a lone teenager, chubby-cheeked and chubby-fingered, stood behind a counter in front of two grimy microwaves with a look of bottomless boredom in his eyes, and I said, "No, I'll probably just wait till I get there."

"Well, alrighty," my father said. He spread his arms, and when we hugged, he pulled me into him, pressing my nose into his sternum.

I had the good fortune to ride uncompanioned for the first hour. I looked out the window at the drab landscape, the switchgrass and softwoods giving way to the occasional golf course or go-cart track. I tried to sleep, gave up, and opened the volume of Zola. With a mechanical pencil, I underlined the word *betteraves*—"chard," according to the dictionary, but I didn't know what chard was either; *rafale*—"gust," which I tried vainly to write in the margins amid the bus's constant buckling and swaying across the lanes, producing what looked like a child's line drawing of waves; and so on with the French words for "sweep," "swamp," "lash," and "slope," until, after two pages, tedium overwhelmed me, and I leaned my temple against the headrest to study the luxuriant gray hairs growing from a crusty mole on the neck of the man across the aisle.

In Marietta, a lone customer got in: thirty, perhaps, wiry and wide-eyed, with chapped lips and droopy jeans held up tenuously by a braided leather belt. I looked away when he caught sight of me, but he sat beside me anyway, saying "Scuse me," to which I replied "No problem" before opening to an arbitrary page of Zola to stare assiduously at a paragraph that might have described a ruined church. At one of the countless local stops, my seatmate asked if I had a cigarette.

"I don't, sorry."

"You don't smoke?"

"Yeah, I just don't have any on me."

"Aight. I got that."

He must have sensed in this exchange familiarity sufficient to encumber me with many details about his life. He had been in the military, he said, and had gone into business after getting out. I didn't ask what sort of business. "Urban greeting cards," he said after a moment. "Like Hallmark, you know, but real-life stuff. We got a couple hang-ups we gotta get through real quick, but it won't be long before we take off."

"See, I got a gal, right," he continued unbidden. "I stay with her right now, she my business partner, too. But she's like a little reluctant, you know? Like it's a business, you don't get out what you don't put in, you gotta spend money to make money, she need to understand that."

"Sure."

"Right. Exactly. And that's her role in this thing. I said that to her, I said you got the money end, I got the product, the creative part. You wanna hear some of my poems?"

Possessed neither of the indulgence to say *mm-hm* nor of the cruelty to say *mh-mm*, I opted for a protracted *mmmm* that might be interpreted as assent or refusal, and my neighbor took it according to his inclinations, sliding a scuffed sheet of blue notebook paper folded into an envelope from his back pocket. As he did, I noticed neat rows of horizontal scars, fifteen or twenty of them, descending the undersides of his forearms.

"Greeting cards, I told you that, right? So like the idea is, they gonna rhyme, we gonna take Mother's Day, Father's Day, all the big holidays, and we gonna have poems to go with them."

He began to recite.

"*I bet you mad you haven't heard from me, but I would never forget our anniversary. You know you the most important person in my life, and I'll always be glad I made you my wife.* What you think?"

"Might work."

"*When no one else would hold me down, Mom, you was always around. Through good and bad, through thick and thin, I always knew you was my friend.* Then there's this other one: *I remember when you was my little man. Now I can't believe how tall you stand. I watched you before you could even crawl, and knew back then you could do it all. You held your head up through frustration, so let me tell you congratulations. I'm so glad you made it to your graduation.* I wrote that one for my son, he seventeen now. I got that one on the back burner, I may not publish that one, I'm gonna break it out just for him."

His material exhausted, he turned to his side as though to nap, but jerked every five or ten minutes. With a look of urgency, he unzipped his duffel bag, plugged an earpiece into a portable radio, and began conversing with some figure in his imagination.

"Hey," he said, "what? Nah. I can't do that . . . I ain't even around right now . . . What you . . . I'm in New York. Damn straight I'm in New York. They flew me up here. I got a business meeting. I told you I had people."

Just then the driver came over the loudspeaker: "Ladies and gentlemen, we are now entering Atlanta, Georgia. Atlanta, Georgia, folks, this is the last and final stop for this coach. If you are traveling onward please look for your destination on the screens to the right when you enter the station."

"I *did* say New York. I'm flying out of Atlanta. Once they let me off here I gotta get a cab to the airport . . . "

Inevitably, my hoped-for decampment was barred by the passengers in the forward rows, who seemed, like all passengers, to have entered a lull as the bus glided between the yellow lines of the bay, and could only stand, gather their things, and shuffle out in lumbering perplexity. "Hey, man, you mighta heard me sayin' I gotta get to the airport, don't think you could hook me up with twenty bucks for the taxi?" the poet asked, wrapping the cord around his radio and tucking it in his back pocket. I said, as with the cigarettes, I didn't have anything on me.

I reached Fox's town three hours later, at dusk. No more than ten people remained in the bus: a few students with huge cloth bags full of laundry from home, older people going to or returning from a family visit. Fox was standing in the vestibule waiting. She had on polyester track pants, a baby tee, and glitter over her eyelids. She smiled, then kissed me on the lips when I reached her.

"I brought something for you," I said, kneeling to unzip my backpack and extracting a yellow rose from the gas station where my father had filled up that morning. The stem was kinked and oozing thin sap.

"How sweet of you. We'll hold a funeral for it when we get home."

"Where is home?"

"Uptown. It's like eight blocks from here. I didn't tell my roommate you're coming, I'm going to pretend I just met you out and we're hooking up. It's easier than asking permission."

"Maybe you should get your own place. I don't feel like you have the best of luck with roommates."

"You live with your dad."

"Touché."

"You ready for some rasslin'?" she asked.

"I assumed you were kidding."

"God, why do you talk like that? *I assyumed you weh kidding.* I'm broke and I *assyume* you are too and this is something to do besides sit in my bedroom listening to my roommate watch rom-coms at full blast."

"I missed you," I said, turning to her and grabbing her hands.

"Tss," she said, grinning and batting her big eyes, and tugged me forward.

After we dropped off my things, we walked to the gymnasium of a high school bordering the river. Past the gravel lot half-full of pickups and beaters stood a cyclone fence where an obese late adolescent was taking tickets in a gownlike T-shirt emblazoned with the words FUCK YOU, WE'RE THE ELIMINATORS. "Hi," Fox said to him, "we're a plus-two for Kurt Krush."

The doorman picked up a clipboard resting on a concrete block placed upright, asked Fox for her name, scratched it off the list, and handed us each a plastic snap-on bracelet.

"Kurt Krush," I snickered.

"You don't have to have fun," Fox said, "but you can't leave."

The sound in the gymnasium was like harsh wind whipping an awning. Two hundred or so people were there, some on wooden risers, another sixty or seventy in folding chairs on the floor. Fox squeezed my fingers and said, "Don't get excited, but we're in the second row. VIP, baby."

In the ring, at one of the turnbuckles, an olive-skinned man in a black spandex singlet that left one nipple exposed was pretending to bite the ear of his contender, who screamed in mock agony. A cluster of spectators had stood up to give him the finger; he looked at one, said, "Fuck you, redneck," and spat in his direction. The referee, a drab man with a neck beard and a whistle between his lips, grabbed his shoulder, urging him to stop showboating and return to the match, but the wrestler shoved him back and he fell to the floor unconscious. Many spectators yelled desperately for him to turn around while his adversary, with a lusty grin, nodded slowly and drew a blackjack from his tights. After he had snuck up, tapped his preening foe, and knocked him out with a blow to the jaw, the referee revived with a start and gave a three count to mingled shouts of jubilation and despair.

The event dragged on until nearly midnight. There were two tag teams of Mexican wrestlers, each composed of a protagonist with a dwarf-sized version of himself: Demonio

Rojo one was called, and his partner Mini-Demonio. Jeers met a Japanese man in flamboyant bell-bottoms embroidered with dragons: "Hiroshima," "Hirohito," they yelled, along with other unintelligible, vaguely Oriental-sounding combinations of syllables. He was pelted with plastic beer cups after he blinded his opponent, spitting green mist into his face. When he walked back to the locker room holding the belt he had defended, a drunk man, very thin, with concrete spatters on his buckskin boots, shouted, "Eat shit, you goddamn firework-makin' motherfucker."

An obscene chant accompanied a dweeb in a tuxedo who climbed into the ring to announce the main event. He had said only a few words when a heavy metal song interrupted him, and Fox's customer stepped out from behind the curtain.

"That's him," she said.

"Is he famous?" I asked her.

"The fuck should I know?"

When he was ringside, walking past the fans and giving them high fives, Fox grabbed my hand, raised it high, and screamed, "Get him, Kurt!" The man was six and a half feet tall, his arms thick as the whole rib eyes we got in at work before the kitchen managers cut them down, weird veins swelling spontaneously over his muscles as he moved.

"I'm supposed to protect you from that guy's advances?" I asked her.

"He's nice," Fox said. "I think he's just lonely. If he sees me with you, he'll chill."

Once in the ring, Kurt flung back his blond curls from his shoulders, made devil horns with each of his extended hands, and bellowed into the air like a werewolf. The fans, already knowing the challenger, hissed and catcalled no sooner than the announcer said, "And hailing from the mean streets of Harlem, New York . . . " Over the collective derision, it was impossible to make out his name. The bassline of a rap song boomed through the PA, and a black man stepped out in a chinchilla coat and Cazal glasses, leaning on a jewel-encrusted cane. With him was a curvy woman in a red leather catsuit. The fans pointed at her and chanted, "She's got herpes," to which her presumptive pimp responded with a grandiose show of outrage.

They switched to "Crush him, Kurt," when he draped the coat across the valet's arms and leapt over the top rope into the ring. Kurt's specialty seemed to be a backhand across the chest, which he dealt ten times in a row, with the crowd shouting "Woo!" to each one. Throughout, Kurt had the advantage, at one point even throwing the pimp through a folding table outside the ring. He dragged him into the crowd, they punched back and forth, blood draining over their faces, and from up close, a band of vertical cuts was visible on each man's forehead. When Kurt hurled him back into the ring by his braids, the pimp shed real tears and begged for mercy, and Kurt turned around and laughed, seeking advice from the audience, who clamored for him to deal the final blow. Satisfied, he looked back and began stomping the mat in preparation for some sort of attack; as he did so, the referee looked away, trying to bring order to the crowd, and the pimp's valet jumped up behind the ropes and struck Kurt in the head with the cane. The pimp rolled Kurt onto his back, and three seconds later had secured his victory, with the announcer shouting, "Ladies and gentlemen, the winner and still reigning champion: Cocoa White!" Kurt's cronies rushed the ring to avenge him, and the pimp's associates came out to fend them off, white versus black, leather pants and vests versus bandanas and basketball jerseys.

"Let's try to beat the rush," Fox said, jogging off toward the door. Then, a minute later, when we had made it to an under-built, semi-residential street: "So, what did you think?"

"Mystifying," I said.

"For God's sake."

At her home, she opened a bottle of prosecco and filled two bulbous glasses painted garishly with moons and stars. She dimmed the lights, lit a candle, put music on the tape deck; these clichés of romance felt no less romantic for being clichés because I had not ceased to be infatuated with her. When I licked her, she groaned curtly, as if from a sharp pain, covered my ears with her hands, and said, "If you keep this up, I might not let you go home."

I stayed with her for two more nights: happy ones, in essence, and we spoke tentatively of my returning there to live with her. It was not so much a lack of love as a lack of imagination that made me refuse; failing to grasp why I'd been so miserable before, I was unable to see how I might live with her in another way. My return bus left at eight on Monday morning; I set the alarm on my watch for six. She barely woke when I kissed her goodbye, her words and the way she hugged me still had about them the volatility of dreams. I walked to the bus station alone. At the diner across the street, I ordered a coffee to go, and stood drinking it a while at the counter, looking up words from *Germinal*.

16

One weekend morning over breakfast—fried eggs and bacon and an oat shake for my father, coffee with milk for myself—my father asked, "How would you feel about going to visit your aunt?" This was a woman I hadn't seen in years.

When I was a child, she sometimes caught the bus to my mother's house, or had herself driven there by a boyfriend or husband in the black car she'd inherited from her father—"Oh, dear God, kill me now," my mother used to whisper as she watched it park through the living room window. My aunt had an anxiety disorder, I'd always been told, and that was why she never learned to drive. Her thin hair was the pale yellow of old linens, and she had delicate, dappled skin like a withered fruit. She would come in without knocking and seat herself in the wicker rocker beside the shelf that held my mother's record collection. Her legs didn't reach the ground, and she had to lean forward then back with her torso to set it in motion. "You're not busy, are you?" she always asked, in a manner that seems on reflection to have concealed some sort of insult; my mother would sigh and say, "Never a moment's rest." But by then, my aunt had already begun to gossip about my father: his grades, his requests for money, how he never came to visit; or she'd decry the defects of her boyfriends or husbands, whom we never saw, except through the windshield of her father's car, and even then, we could make out nothing particular about any of them, as they all wore identical long black beards. My aunt would bemoan the hardship of caring for her mother, who needed to eat better and get out more; and inevitably she would take out a pamphlet soliciting donations for some endangered species of fowl and leave it on the bookshelf by the door. There was little pretense to dialogue; her grievances were like a catechism, and once she'd recited them, she was impatient to go. Then she would rock frantically until the chair tipped far enough forward that she could roll her weight out onto her feet. "Next time I'm going to buy you a smaller one of these," she always said before walking out.

I'd always heard my aunt had been a rebellious teenager. The night after her mother's funeral, when I joined her in her attic to look for keepsakes for my father, I found a wooden sign on which she had written, "Home is no good for me." She said she used to hold it out on the roadside when she hitchhiked. Her parents sent her to a private school, and my father apparently resented her for it, feeling his own public high school beneath him; but she lasted only a few years before they expelled her for smoking marijuana in the bathroom. My mother called her a hippie, but I never heard her express any opinion about world peace, racism, global warming, or the redistribution of wealth; she seemed unconcerned with, even unaware of, much beyond her family. She lived most of the time in her childhood bedroom, moving out whenever she met a man or managed to keep the same job for more than three months; after her father died, she convinced her mother to pay for an addition to the house, where she could have a kitchen and a private bathroom;

when her mother died in turn, she inherited the house, ostensibly because she had cared for her parents while my father had left to chase his ambitions, but probably because they'd been afraid she'd wind up living on the street. "That's what I get for growing up," was my father's lament whenever he mentioned it.

My aunt seemed never to have passed into adulthood. My mother said she had been addicted to drugs throughout her twenties, had run with bikers and lowlifes, and had never given serious thought to supporting herself. She was arrested once for dealing, but an alternative sentencing program allowed her to pursue a master's degree instead of going to prison. In a penitent moment, she chose criminology, saying she understood how good people could fall into wayward circumstances. After graduating, she took a post at a mental hospital, but left within a few days. "I can't stand to be around those people," she told my mother, and ever since she had worked as a cocktail waitress or cashier when not unemployed.

I knew my father was not asking whether I wanted to see my aunt; I doubt anyone could. Even on her last visit, five or six years before, she had begun to stammer unnervingly, and could barely manage a conversation. I didn't know my father's feelings about his sister; he had never talked to me about his childhood with her, or about anything else, really; but I guessed there must be something upsetting to him in her decline that he preferred not to witness on his own. I said yes. I looked into the disk of light tipping back and forth on the surface of my coffee, which reflected the stubble on my cheeks and chin. My father rolled a strip of bacon into a tube and ran it along the rim of his plate to catch the last of the congealed yellow egg yolk before eating it.

My aunt's house was forty-five minutes away, on the top of a mountain. We went there on a clear day, cool but not cold, "a fine day for a drive," people would have said in the past. My father listened to public radio. Not only did he hear his own views echoed there, I believe he thought the broadcast's theme would appeal to me as well, and even lead to a conversation between us about the hypocrisy of the Republican Party, the depletion of the ozone layer, or the lamentably low percentage of Americans who spoke a second language. But I was scandalized by none of this, and sat there in silence, thinking that indignation was, after all, a quite pleasurable end in itself and not the goad to action it was commonly imagined to be. The day's programming featured an expert on *enlightened progressives*, a group of people distinguished by inclinations toward recycling, traditional medicine, Eastern philosophy, and pacifism. During a break, a song played, called "Me and Billy the Kid," the supposed recollections, set in rhyme, of a colleague of the famous bandit, and, unable to imagine why such a song had ever been written—anyway, I had always hated folk music and almost anything composed for the guitar—I began to wriggle in irritation and stuck a finger in my right ear, whereas my father, who had played piano in a honky-tonk group in college, tapped the steering wheel with his flattened hands and turned his head to one side during an appealing passage, lowering his ear toward the speaker like a robin listening for worms beneath the soil.

His sister's house, fir-green, lay hidden behind trees and bushes only partially and badly pruned. It was one floor with a copper roof, of a style vaguely evocative of the Usonian homes built by Frank Lloyd Wright in the 1940s, and must have looked fashionable when it was built. Around it ran a row of bricks enclosing a former garden. Odd tools lay in the yard, rusting around a birdbath full of sedimented leaves, and hummingbird feeders hung from looped screws under the eaves. We walked across stepping-stones that sank in the damp mud, onto a welcome mat made of strips of tire rubber, and my father rang the bell.

"Oh!" my aunt called, her shadow traversing the bottle-glass window. After unlatching the chain and turning the dials of the various locks, she opened the door. My father's eyes scanned the bookshelves, the fake elephant foot filled with umbrellas, and the half-finished dollhouse on the console in the anteroom. "Well who is this, then?" my aunt said, pretending not to recognize me. She was thinner than when I'd last seen her, despite her sagging potbelly, and her dress was at once so shoddy and so eccentric as to suggest utter isolation from the company of others. I was expected to joke back, then we could all share a chuckle, but instead, from petulance or a want of ingenuity, I stood and said nothing until she turned her back and guided us inside. We walked past the fireplace, now sealed with an aluminum plate, on the elaborate iron grating of which I had slit open my eyebrow when I was four, past the dining room lined with shelves packed with florid old china and a painting of a glass bottle and lemon in a burlap frame, into the kitchen. My aunt sat in a red vinyl booth from a diner, purchased from an antique dealer; on the table in front of it were newspaper clippings and a black-and-white television with the sound turned down. My father stayed standing and crossed his arms. I sat on a folding step stool.

"You look skinny," my aunt said disapprovingly.

"I've been working out," my father said. "I'm not skinny, I'm getting in shape."

"What?" my aunt squawked, in incomprehension or disdain.

"I said, I'm working out. I'm exercising. I'm trying to take better care of myself."

My aunt glowered at my father. It seemed to me obvious that she was deranged, or far along the road to derangement, and her thoughts hinged only partly on the world as it lay before her. She turned to me and said, "And you look like you're going to up and blow away." I stared down at my bony arms. They wore a coat of thin, evenly distributed hairs and were sand-brown from the elbow down and corpse-white from the elbow up. I crossed them, wrapping my ribs in my hands, and looked at the wire cage, stuffed with suet, that dangled outside the window and from which a squirrel hung inverted by its feet, eagerly snacking.

My aunt and father talked about old friends, acquaintances, and family members who were dying or had already died. Their names rang a bell, but I had met none of them that I could remember, except for a great-uncle who had succumbed to cancer. My aunt asked my father to make her a whiskey and water, and he did, in an exotic vessel shaped like a clepsydra that left the liquids in two layers. My aunt's eyes grew glassy as she drank, and though she appeared to talk to my father, her attention lingered increasingly over the silently screaming faces of the game show contestants on TV. The gaps in her speech grew longer, and her responses less and less germane. Frustrated, my father asked her to accompany him to the dining room, where they could talk in private.

"What?" she asked after a failed attempt at processing his request.

"Good God," my father said, taking his glasses by the bridge and propping them on his furrowed forehead. Looking down at the clippings strewn on the table, he drew in a breath.

"I said," he repeated, each syllable stern and resounding, as though spoken for a foreigner or an inattentive subordinate, "will-you-come-to-the-dining-room-for-a-second-please-so-I-can-talk-to-you-in-private."

"You don't have to scream," my aunt screamed. My father took her elbow, pressed the flat of his other hand into her lower back to help her from the booth, and led her away.

When I heard the wooden chairs creak, I stood and tiptoed to the doorframe. My father was trying to explain the contest to her. He told her how much fat he'd lost, how much weight he was able to lift. He was competing against thousands of entries, he said. People who were younger, with better genetics, who didn't have jobs and could devote themselves to working out seven days a week. He was pulled in every direction, he said, between the divorce and his profession and trying to take care of me.

"Why do you want to do a contest?" my aunt asked. "I don't think you'll become a bodybuilder at this age. Why don't you just worry about keeping your job and trying to hold onto a woman for once?"

I could hear my father suck his teeth in reply. "I'm not becoming a fucking bodybuilder," he said. "Will you just listen to me for a second?" Then, more softly, he continued: "This is very important to me. I'm not asking for much, I just need a thousand dollars. Dad and Mom never said no to you when they were around. Besides, I can pay you back in two weeks. It's the photographer, he won't book me a session unless I put down a deposit in advance, and things are a little bit tight. It's the photographer and a couple of other things—glycerol, posing oil, a last batch of supplements. I must be pretty close to the top of the pile—I just can't believe there's that many people out there my age that are putting in this kind of effort—but the photos . . . you can do anything with them. I saw this one guy, his photos were five minutes apart, and in one he looks like a total schlub and in the other he's like goddamn Arnold Schwarzenegger. If the lighting is off or the angles are wrong, you can look short, skinny, fat, all your definition can up and disappear. Imagine I put in all this effort and then lose because I was pinching pennies at the last moment."

"Get the checkbook," my aunt said. My father walked to the end table beneath the rotary phone and slid open the drawer, the handles of which were carved in the shape of chestnuts, at the same time as I slipped past him, saying, "I've got to go to the bathroom." This was not true, and once I had shut the door behind me, I wasted minutes looking at the salves, bath salts, hand tools, and enemas beneath the sink, as well as the many bottles of pills behind the sliding mirror, and then pressing down on the air-filled cushion of the toilet seat, for hemor- rhoids, I assumed. When I came out, the transaction was done. My father took my aunt's hand, held it, and told her he loved her, and afterward I kissed her cheek and her dry hair pressed into my face. My father left with a shifty expression, the folded check between two fingers, and shrugged mock stoically as he caught my eye. He tried to discuss his impressions of my aunt's deterioration, which did seem to portend an approaching col- lapse. He didn't covet the house or the money, but it hurt him that his parents hadn't remembered him in their wills, it hurt him to know that his sister had come away with everything by refusing all responsibility in the world beyond their family. He was gloomy as we always are when death encroaches on those close to us, or those who once were—his sister, but also the people he and she had spoken of, and about whom I knew nothing. "Rodney," my father said, a name I'd never heard before, "he used to sit by me in orchestra, last I heard of him he was doing great, he was a retail broker, he made money hand over fist. His wife wakes up one day and he's not moving. Brain aneurysm." I was not disposed to talk, being now depressed myself and wishing, in silence, to see my impressions of my aunt through to their end, as I used often to want to do when I thought the things I felt possessed logical rather than merely temporal finitude, and *could* somehow be thought to their end; and so after he had uttered three or four such ruminations, and I had maintained silence throughout, we drove the rest of the way without speaking, the prattle of public radio nearly inaudible over the cold air sweeping the cracked windows.

Less than a week after our visit, a postman rang at the door. It was midmorning, and my father was at work. I signed the screen of his device with a plastic stylus and was handed an almost weightless box from a veterinary company with the head of a stolid-looking steer as a logo. I left it on the table in the dining room, really only half of the L-shaped room with the sectional sofa against the back wall, and went back to the television to finish a documentary about two women with Diogenes syndrome.

"Oh, nice!" my father said when he returned home. He rushed to the kitchen, swinging his arms, to retrieve scissors. I asked what it was.

"Well, ha, ha, you're probably going to think your old man's lost his damned mind. It's called Finaplix. Trenbolone acetate. It's a cattle steroid. They give it to heifers to beef them up before slaughter."

"And what are you going to do with it?"

"The same thing the cows do, basically. If it'll make a cow big, it'll make a man big. I'm hoping to put on another ten pounds before the contest is over. As far as the specifics, I printed the directions off the internet at work, we'll see whether I screw it up or not. What I've got here is a couple dozen pellets. For cattle, they've got this gun kind of thing, they shoot them right under their skin and the pellets time-release, so there's a constant supply of the stuff in their system. As you can guess, I'm not wild about the idea of shooting something the size of a pea into one of my ass cheeks, but for human use, you can crush it up, dissolve it in alcohol, run it through a coffee filter, then mix it in sterilized vegetable oil. Once you do that, it's injectable, and it's no different from the pharmaceutical stuff. But since it's veterinary grade, there's a loophole, and it's 100 percent legal."

"Is it safe?"

My father didn't have to worry about his hair—for the most part, it was gone—but I imagined his testicles shrinking to the size of raisins, barely visible in their empty sac, or crocodilian acne creeping over his arms and back.

"It's fine. You know, this country is so goddamn puritanical. Between tobacco and alcohol you've got almost five hundred thousand deaths a year nationwide, and people are up in arms about steroids. I mean, even Nathaniel Sweezey, the guy who runs Paradigm Fitness, admitted to taking them back when he was on the pro circuit. Mark McGuire—he can say what he wants about legal supplements, you don't end up with twenty-two-inch pipes taking anything you can get over the counter. Now I know steroids aren't quote 'good' for you, but neither is coffee, neither are fatty foods, this whole country is full of land whales and nobody's talking about banning Fritos . . . I look at it like everything else. You do it intelligently, carefully, and you can minimize the risk. I've been reading up on what to do to minimize the effects: you take milk thistle to protect the liver, *Tribulus terrestris* to block the estrogen conversion, drink lots of water, and try to eat clean. I'm just looking to do a short cycle, after that I'll probably never touch the stuff again."

"Don't they test the finalists?"

"I'll cross that bridge when I come to it. Let's be honest—I realize I'm probably not going to win. There's too many contestants, too many factors outside my control. I'm a fifty-five-year-old man. I think I look pretty damned good compared to most people my age, but I realize I'm no Steve Reeves."

"Maybe you'll get extra points for the essay?"

"It's a possibility," my father said. "They act like that's a big part of the final score. But you saw the movie: that guy with AIDS busted his ass harder than anyone, and they still chose someone else. The main thing is, they're trying to sell supplements. If you've got me and you've got some kid that's shredded to the bone, who are you going to pick? Anyhow, supposing I did win . . . there's got to be some way to game the system. They supposedly test in the NFL, and you'd have a hard time convincing me a 350-pound defensive lineman is just drinking protein shakes and eating lots of steak."

My father urged me to start going with him to the gym. "You can't believe what it does for you," he said, "just knowing you've already gotten something done before the day's even really started." He must have had some sense that I wasn't well in those days, I'd told him as much, had said that I was listless, friendless, with no sense of my future. I'd never played a sport in high school or college, nor had I admired the weird physiques of those who did, but I thought perhaps there would be other benefits to rising early, to adopting some discipline, whatever its nature, and I told him yes.

That evening, he took me to an outlet store to buy workout clothes and a pair of fingerless gloves. For the next few weeks, until the end of the contest, which coincided with my midterms, he would wake me up every morning at 5:30, leaving a cup of coffee on my dresser. I would lie still while he showered and shaved, then wash my face before leaving. We would stop for breakfast at the Waffle House, where I would have a patty melt and my father chicken and eggs. At first, with no sense of what to do, I would walk from machine to machine, copying the movements of the anatomical illustrations stamped on the gray plastic signs affixed to them. The "target muscle group" on the figures in the pictures, always hairless, always male, was indicated with a small oval. I performed one action for each, then sat near the entrance and waited for my father to finish.

As much as his routine and his reputed sense of well-being, what my father enjoyed about the gym was the opportunity for gossip. Since his return, he had made no friends I knew of—doubtless the divorce hadn't helped—and the ones from his high school and college days were busy with their jobs and families. He was not one to talk about work, and wanted to forget, I think, all that had happened with Karen. The gym was a small society he could observe with the interest of a gardener following the progress of his plants in the growing season. There were two short brothers, stout and neckless, Jesse and Aaron, who dealt steroids to the amateur bodybuilders and powerlifters and their hangers-on; a lean, foppish doctor with bleached hair and bleached eyebrows who "sponsored" a number of young, athletic men whom he invited to his lake house for lurid parties; a woman I couldn't stop looking at, with globoid silicone breasts and solid, shapely legs, who worked out in high-top sneakers and a bikini stamped with the American flag; a reedy, swarthy man my father called "this jerkoff," who would stand outside smoking cigarettes until his partner showed up, then don a bench press shirt, a polyester contraption that pulled his arms forward and up like a mummy's, and linger around assorted pieces of equipment, taking long rest periods and preventing anyone else from using them.

The trenbolone gave my father insomnia. After midnight, a faint amber haze from the lamp in the living room would arc under my door. Sometimes I could hear him turning the pages of a book, sometimes, softly, the abysmal television broadcast at that hour—horror films, infomercials, or prurient talk shows—and often he would take hour-long walks on the roadside. If he saw a deer or opossum, he would report it with delight the next day.

The effects of the drug were soon apparent. A flushed face, from elevated blood pressure, was his only adverse reaction. For the rest, he looked more compact, harder, drier. He weighed himself each morning on a digital scale in the bathroom and recorded the figure on a tidy chart taped to the wall. Every week, he paid to have his body fat checked in a hydrostatic tank. His weight had varied little—he had dropped three pounds since the contest's beginning—but by his calculations he had lost twenty pounds of fat and replaced the better part of it with lean muscle.

The training programs in his magazines he derided as "bullshit," and he would mock the most complicated ones, which involved arcane equations based on maximum lifts that varied from one week to the next, sometimes over the course of months. "I'm supposed to believe this guy came up with this system, he looks like he can barely add," my father would say, and show me a photo of a hulking, sweat-beaded mass in a red thong. "Supposedly all these pros sign a contract and the companies can publish any article they want under their name. The same goes for the endorsements—they probably don't even know what these products they're advertising are." His cynicism did not prevent his reading these same routines with devotion, and he purchased several issues per month of *Flex* and *Muscle and Fitness* in addition to *Total Body Development.* Occasionally he developed a fascination with one or another of the musclemen, none of whom I could tell apart. "Look at that tricep development," my father would say, laying a centerfold across the table, especially impressed with something he referred to as the *lateral head.* "That guy is just fucking massive."

Soon I could identify my father's heroes: Lee Priest, the short Australian with Superman's shield tattooed on his shoulder; Paul Dillett, the horrifying Canadian with his gap-toothed, cannibalistic smile; reigning Mr. Olympia, Ronnie Coleman, whose back resembled a beetle's shell and who always tucked his briefs into his ass crack to reveal the scalloped striations in his buttocks.

My father asked me to accompany him one weekend to an amateur bodybuilding show in Dalton, Georgia. The German Nightmare, Markus Rühl, would be posing. "It's off-season," my father said, "he must weigh like 350 pounds right now." As the finish grew closer, and the possibility of gaining more muscle or losing more fat diminished, my father took a greater interest in the aesthetics of the sport, and thought he might learn something about posing technique that would make his photos stand out from the others.

The drive down was dispiriting. From my father's quiet neighborhood, we entered a highway cutting through a range of hills, bordered by a thirty-foot concrete wall. We passed the downtown, with its three or four towers and shuttered factories clustered around it, then entered into an endless, ramshackle commercial district with hundreds of raised signs and billboards. It was stuffy in the car, and my father turned on the air conditioning.

"I reckon when you heard your old man was moving down here, you didn't imagine it would be like this," he said.

"Like what?"

"Oh, you know. The thing with the contest. I mean, one minute I'm introducing you to a complete stranger and saying here's my new wife, I was naïve enough to think you guys would like each other, that she could be a real stepmother for you, and then the next thing you know that's all gone and here I am ordering cattle implants and meeting women online and trying to win the Body You Choose competition. You can't call that normal."

"I hadn't really thought about it," I said. "It's not like I had any real expectations."

He apologized again for his absence in my childhood, for having thought about himself when he should have thought of me. "I guess I always had the idea that at some point everything would be perfect, that my job would be settled, my home, my love life, and then I'd have time for the rest, but it doesn't seem to ever happen that way," he said.

"It's fine," I told him, unable to arrive at a more comprehensive or sympathetic response. When signs for carpet mills appeared, he lifted himself from the seat and removed a folded piece of paper from his pocket, a map he had downloaded from

MapQuest. I guided him, turn by turn, the rest of the way, past trailers, houses, and churches with white medal siding and Readerboard signs with waggish admonishments—*Tired of the darkness, follow the Son*, and so forth—to the civic center where the event would take place. There were ten or twenty cars and twenty or thirty pickup trucks in the lot.

My father paid our admission at the ticket window, and we walked over to the trophy room. Amid crisp black-and-white and blurry color photos of track, football, and wrestling teams stood men with the insignia of local gyms embroidered on the breast pockets of their polos, selling T-shirts with Atlas-like figures breaking chains or dinosaurs lifting bent barbells and legends like *Unleash the Beast*. In robes, or with a towel over their shoulders, the competitors milled around and chatted with their acquaintances or wives. Their spray tans stopped a half-inch below their hairlines, and most had missed their eyelids, the backs of their ears, and the interstices between their fingers, so that, from up close, they looked filthy, like miners or wanderers lost in the desert.

My father wanted to sit down early so we would have a decent view of the stage. He used the extra time to call a work acquaintance. The coming week would be a stressful one, he said. His conversation consisted mostly of abbreviations and nicknames referring to procedures and people in authority, and I had no idea what it was about. After ten minutes, the lights went low and the sponsor, the owner of a local feed and seed warehouse, stepped out with a microphone to introduce the athletes.

The differences between them were extreme. Some were barely bigger than I, and their satiny briefs with the number pinned on gave the impression of an ill-advised costume.

165

Others were zit-spangled behemoths, with shaved heads or thinning, bleach-blond hair, their bodies broad heaps of hard protrusions. The music was of a type reserved for such spectacles: excruciating bass drum every three seconds with five high notes on a synthesizer repeated ad nauseam.

After the finalists were announced, Markus Rühl came out to disparate claps and cheers. The floorboards of the stage bowed under his feet. He did not look human, or not exactly. When he planted his fists into his ribs and flared, the wing muscles under his arms nearly touched his elbows. Though each knurl of his complex abdomen protruded beneath his paper-thin skin, when he turned sideways, his stomach bulged like a tortoise shell. "Organ swelling," my father said. "They get it from all the insulin and growth hormone. That'll never go away."

"You're not worried about that?"

"Nah. I can't afford HGH. You're talking a grand a week for what these guys take. If anything, the trenbolone leans you out."

The majority of the audience seemed to be friends and family of the men on stage, and the fans of those eliminated left after the guest posing. When the top four came out for the second round, the auditorium was nearly empty. There was little doubt as to who would win: one man in his twenties, his oiled hair in a ponytail, black dots from his depilated body hair slightly welted over his chest and belly, cast a shadow over the other three. This did not keep the underdogs' supporters from crying foul when the results were announced. My father motioned for us to leave while the winner gave a victory speech, so we could beat the traffic, thin as it would be, out of the lot.

"So what did you think?" he asked, once we'd turned onto the main road.

"It was something different," I said.

"Yeah, that's for sure. Kind of weird, right?"

"They all looked like they'd been cooked in one of those spinning hot dog ovens," I said.

My father laughed, and we drove the rest of the way in silence.

18

As the contest neared its end, my father's account of his own life, once a concatenation of anecdotes and modest excurses and misgivings, dwindled to the pure abstraction of numbers and initialisms, the combinations of which expressed his sense of triumph or dejection at the moment of telling: he was alarmed by his BMI, which ranged between 25 and 27, though he had read BMI wasn't a trustworthy measure of fitness; he experimented with 5×5 workouts, as espoused by strength coach Charles Poliquin, and the HIT system, in which he lost interest after reading how its founder, Mike Mentzer, a libertarian and follower of Ayn Rand, had taken off running naked through the streets and prophesying the end of the world. For someone who'd known my father before his diet, he would have been unrecognizable from the neck down, save for the gray scar on his right forearm, where he'd had a mermaid tattoo from his tour in the navy removed. Nancy started coming over on the weekends, and on Fridays, when she walked through the door, she would tell him how *buff* he looked. "Nonsense," my father would answer.

Every day, he asked me to snap a roll of pictures with a disposable camera and drop it off at the pharmacy for one-hour development. Although the changes in his physique were evident and maybe even commendable, the photos only under-scored his dissimilarity to the bodybuilders in his magazines: he was always too white, too flat, and too small. It was his height, I said to him, that put him at a disadvantage; at six feet four, he was taller than most competitors, so his gains were more spread out. "It's true," he said, "by nature I'm an ectomorph, I was thin all the way into my thirties." I also worried that the poses he was imitating were designed to display, rather than conceal, the defects in a bodybuilder's physique: when he flexed his back, his nipples sagged and his belly poked out, and the lateral postures meant to highlight the development in his legs made him look somehow incontinent. "Just stand naturally," I said, "or maybe with one hand on the doorframe." I was thinking of the outdoor shots his magazines sometimes featured, in which a man with what looked like wires beneath his skin, in faded jeans and reflective sunglasses, would lean a massive arm against a sunstruck rock face, or pull up on the crossbar of a fence. But his face bothered me too, its expression of bare desperation veiled by a factitious smile. His pallor was the real problem, he said—"you notice black guys always look more muscular"—and to remedy it, he started tanning in the afternoons.

When the last day came, he rose early, picked up the paper from the driveway, and zipped it into his duffel bag—it had to be visible in the final photographs, to confirm the date. He complained of light-headedness while I pulled on a T-shirt in the living room. He hadn't eaten the night before; a fast, he had explained, followed by *carbohydrate loading* a few hours before the shoot, would give a rounder, fuller appearance to his *muscle bellies.* He sat down at the kitchen table with a huge yellow bowl and dumped an entire box of Cinnamon Toast Crunch inside.

He accompanied it with a glass of glycerol, "to pull water into the fibers."

After our coffee we drove to the studio, a brown stucco building with a slanted roof like a tilting wing surrounded by a vast parking lot. There was no receptionist to greet us, and it was several minutes before we found the photographer, in a studio painted completely white, taking pictures of a pair of twins dressed as train conductors. One of them crawled to the edge of the platform, and his father lifted him by the rib cage and placed a toy locomotive in his hand. The photographer said we were early, and my father said he knew that, but he needed time to get ready, was there a place he could change? We followed a hallway to a room with an easy chair where he spent an hour smearing his body with Competition Tan and baby oil, asking me for help with the small of his back. When he had achieved the proper sausage-like darkness and gleam, he slipped on his black bikini briefs.

He scrutinized himself in the full-length mirror, turning his arm out and pulling the skin away from his triceps to assay a last time the growth of the "medial head" of the muscle underneath, then started toward the door. But he stopped before grabbing the knob, felt around in his gym bag, and pulled out an oblong box. It appeared to contain an object of foreign manufacture, and I was not sure the proprietors of the company well understood the implications of the name they had chosen for it: *The Ab-O-Litionist*.

"Maybe this is dumb," my father said, "but my abs . . . I never did manage to get much definition there. Once you get a spare tire, it's with you for life . . . " He opened the box and removed a blue, perforated latex sheet, centering it over his trunk so that the egg-shaped apertures made an approximate outline of the rectus abdominus. Then he made me stand behind him and pull the attached handles. They were greasy, and kept slipping away, and each time, my father said "dammit" before carefully replacing the apparatus until, after five minutes, it had left the desired imprint on his stomach, a six-pack of depressed flesh and extruded fat.

The photographer stood my father in front of a gray screen. For the half-hour that he posed, I sat crosswise in a recliner reading a magazine from months before that lay on the end table. Occasionally the lights would brighten or dim, and I would glance up to see my father, half-snarling and half-beaming, a white shimmer on the crown of his head, neck and forearms shivering with tension. He went through the eight poses established by the International Federation of Bodybuilders: the Front Lat Spread, the Front Double Biceps, the Side Chest, the Rear Lat Spread, the Rear Double Biceps, the Side Triceps, the Vacuum Pose plus Abdominals and Thighs, and the Most Muscular, which required him to jut his jaw forward and flare his elbows at forty-five degrees. The photographer shouted encouragement to him: "Squeeze harder! More intensity!" My father knelt down as he rolled another reel of film into his camera, then stood, his left hand poised next to his hip, and flexed his right arm upward, index finger pointed at the ceiling, reminding me of Prince Adam when he holds his sword into the sky, lightning strikes it, and he turns into He-Man; but instead of He-Man's sculpted shoulders and blond locks, my father had a dull chestnut tonsure and a bit of chub hanging over the elastic of his briefs. "I think that's the one," the photographer said, assuming a tone of confidence and turning off his lights to intimate to my father that the time he had paid for was over. My father disappeared, then returned in a red sweat suit, shook the photographer's hand, and gave him a check. "Well, that's that," he said, and walked out ahead of me, spots of oil seeping into the fabric around his neck, buttocks, and elbows.

Back at home, he looked over the entry form one last time and reread his statement of purpose before sealing both in a manila envelope.

"What are you going to do, now that it's over?" I asked.

"Eat a goddamned lasagna," he said and laughed, "and some ice cream. And drink a six-pack of beer. Ha, ha. Honestly, I don't know. Nancy and I have been thinking about taking a trip. Somewhere cheap, Cancún, Puerto Rico, somewhere like that. I mean, I've done my part, right? I made it through the twelve weeks, nobody can take that from me. I'd love to win, but I probably won't, them's the odds—and in all sincerity, I'd be hard-pressed to give up everything here to go be a fitness consultant in Arizona. I'm happy with my job, I'm happy I can finally be here with you, and I don't remember you ever singing the praises of the Arizona sunsets, I'm happy with the house, and once my finances are together I'll probably look into buying it . . . realistically, all that matters more to me than a shot at being on the cover of a muscle magazine. What's really important is, I had a goal, I saw it through to the end, I didn't give up. And God knows there were times when I wanted to. So, I'll drop these photos in the mail and we'll see what happens from there."

He told me Nancy would be coming that evening and that they were going out for a celebration dinner. He invited me, but I didn't want to accompany them. When they left, I wasted time bathing, looking at old photos, and snooping through my father's dresser, where I found a pack of lambskin condoms and an unusual foreign coin. I watched television, forced down a glass of lukewarm gin, and went to bed. I was only just under the skin of awareness, swaddled in half-thought-half-dreams that faded when I rolled over or drew the sheets onto my shoulders. I was thinking of the future, when I might do something interesting and my life's character would cease to feel provisional and take on what people call meaning or direction. Late, I heard my father stumble in, drunk and giggling. He was telling the last part of a story. "Can you believe that?" he said and cackled. I wanted suddenly very badly to know what he thought might be beyond belief. I woke up morose, thought how each passing moment was unique, how we talk and think about this uniqueness often but do no honor to what it implies, because how?

I did not get out of bed. I'd left a low-budget slasher film in the VCR. Nancy and my father watched part of it, ridiculing the terrible special effects, then replaced it with *Seven Years in Tibet*. I heard them kiss and make pronouncements of love, and before the film was over, they went to sleep.

At three in the morning, I stood up and walked into the living room. The light was left on, and the image of the furnishings was doubled in transparent tones on the sliding glass door. The floor was littered with foil chip bags and crimson soda cans, crimped in the center and lying flat, their concave undersides exposed; a half-eaten tiramisu in a plastic takeout container; Nancy's open suitcase; the blue and white boxes of videocassettes; and other, less memorable testaments to my father's physically more robust but inwardly diminished life.

Dear readers,

As well as relying on bookshop sales, And Other Stories relies on subscriptions from people like you for many of our books, whose stories other publishers often consider too risky to take on.

Our subscribers don't just make the books physically happen. They also help us approach booksellers, because we can demonstrate that our books already have readers and fans. And they give us the security to publish in line with our values, which are collaborative, imaginative and 'shamelessly literary'.

All of our subscribers:

- receive a first-edition copy of each of the books they subscribe to
- are thanked by name at the end of our subscriber-supported books
- receive little extras from us by way of thank you, for example: postcards created by our authors

BECOME A SUBSCRIBER,
OR GIVE A SUBSCRIPTION TO A FRIEND

Visit andotherstories.org/subscriptions to help make our books happen. You can subscribe to books we're in the process of making. To purchase books we have already published, we urge you to support your local or favourite bookshop and order directly from them – the often unsung heroes of publishing.

OTHER WAYS TO GET INVOLVED

If you'd like to know about upcoming events and reading groups (our foreign-language reading groups help us choose books to publish, for example) you can:

- join our mailing list at: andotherstories.org
- follow us on Twitter: @andothertweets
- join us on Facebook: facebook.com/AndOtherStoriesBooks
- admire our books on Instagram: @andotherpics
- follow our blog: andotherstories.org/ampersand

ADRIAN NATHAN WEST grew up in the United States and lives in Spain. He has translated more than twenty books from Spanish, Catalan, and German, among them Rainald Goetz's *Insane*, Pere Gimferrer's *Fortuny*, and Marianne Fritz's *The Weight of Things*. His first book, *The Aesthetics of Degradation*, was published in 2016. His essays and criticism have appeared in the *New York Review of Books*, the *Times Literary Supplement*, and many other journals in print and online.